DEAD LAKE

BY

MURPHY EDWARDS

FOR:

Miss Nancy Hamilton, who taught me about writing.
and
Robert W. Murphy, who taught me about reading. My world is a
smaller place without you in it. I miss you bro.

ACKNOWLEDEGEMENTS

Thanks Gary Lucas and all at Severed Press. In the world of the
undead they are very much alive. When Gary asked me to write a
novel based on their popular Dead Bait Anthologies, I was
flattered. At the time, *Dead Lake* was little more than a few notes
in a ratty journal. Gary encouraged me to feed that 'story germ' a
deadly dose of creepy and bring an undead tale to life.

Ghastly Gar Gills and Ghoulish Grins to Sean T. Page, the true
Minister of Zombies, Dennis 'Doc' Hensley, James Ward Kirk,
Rebecca Besser, Donald White, Kevin Whiteley and all at
Criminal Class Press, Bill Olver at Big Pulp, William Cook at
Bloodsoaked Graphics for the awesome book cover, Midwest
Writers Workshop, Ardetta, The Splatterpunk Saints, The Lord
Above and all my faithful readers.

Two fins up and special thanks to Elisha J. Murphy, my first
reader, an awesome editor and a true believer. You're the best.

Introduction

The Dead Bait anthologies from Severed Press are the slimy benchmark for watery horror. These books have seen everything from mutant crabs to zombie piranha fish, and have contributed to giving thousands of readers a mortal fear of the deep.

Now, here is a novel inspired by these damp tales of terror – the classic pulp horror of Dead Lake is making ominous ripples in the murky water and you'd better do your best to get to dry land as fast as you can swim. Murphy Edwards has taken a classic B-Movie plot and stuffed it full of characters you wouldn't want to be stuck in an elevator with as well as a new set of undead monsters to haunt those sleepless nights.

It's time to grab your badge and join DNR Officer Nickles down by the lake. He's gonna need all the help he can get to deal with the unnatural fishy terror that awaits…

Sean T Page
Ministry of Zombies
Author of: War against the Walking Dead, Metahorde and The Official Zombie Handbook UK

DEAD LAKE

BY

MURPHY EDWARDS

CHAPTER 1

Hearld Money crushed out his cigarette on the heel of his boot and stared out over the rough water of Vivid Valley Lake. A cold wind had kicked up, filling the surface of the water with white caps. The sandy soil under his feet was soaked with thick, blackened blood that sucked at his boot soles like molasses. The steep banks along the shoreline were rutted, the soil plowed deep and thrashed into festering piles of excrement surrounded by puddles of congealed blood. Bits of torn flesh hung from nearby limbs and clung to the mossy rocks. He took a long pull from his hip flask and shoved it back in his pocket.

A heavy mist had crept over the valley and shrouded the lake in thick, gray fog. Money took a step back from the remains and lit a fresh smoke. A small boat appeared in the mist. It was skimming over the water at a dangerous clip, throwing a strong wake and heading straight for the sandy knoll next to Money. He recognized the boat, knew the hull numbers by heart. It was Sgt. Charlie Nickles.

Nickles was out of the boat the minute it bottomed out on the knoll. The smell of weeping tree sap, evergreens and wind-blown pollen mixed with the odors of rotting fish and death. He approached Money, shouting into a cell phone and waving his free hand in the air. "I'm out here now. Won't know much more till I have a look for myself. I'm well aware who made the call. He's standing here in front of me right now. Don't get your shorts in a wad, and don't call me back. I'll call you."

Money leaned in close, hoping to learn who was on the other end of the phone. He caught random bits of the conversation through Nickles' phone, words like 'nutcase', 'whack job', 'public nuisance' and 'drunken pain-in-the-ass', but nothing about the carcass he'd found.

The carcass lay draped over a nearby log. Bones and tufts of bloody hair jutted out of the remains at odd angles. The head, what there was of it, was crushed flat and stripped of its flesh. The stomach and organs had been removed and the legs were snapped like dried twigs. Money tugged at the handkerchief in his jacket and stuffed it over his nose and mouth, a feeble attempt to ward off the stench. He gagged, choking back bile and fighting the urge to lose his liquor-laced breakfast. The smell leached through the thin cotton and crawled up his nostrils.

Nickles clapped his phone shut. "What've you got this time, Money?"

Money pointed at the bloody mess on the log. "See for yourself."

Nickles approached the carcass, waving the stench away from his face with a meaty hand. He was no cherry when it came to death—car crashes, homicides, suicides, maulings, hunting accidents— he'd had a lungful of them all. The stench surrounding him now was a nauseating mixture of cod liver oil and limburger cheese being scorched in a cast iron skillet. It seeped through his freshly-pressed uniform, saturated his flesh, penetrated his pores and gnawed at his soul. He examined the log, removed a ball point pen from his uniform shirt and picked at the

bloody mess.

"What is it?" asked Money.

Nickles flicked the bloody glob off the end of his pen and wiped it clean. "Near as I can tell, a deer, at least it was. Now, it's just a stinkin' pile of rancid meat and gut leavings."

Money stuffed the handkerchief back over his nose and inhaled deeply. He nudged a bloody stone with the toe of his boot. "Looks like a bear got hold of it. That'd be my guess, anyway. That what you're thinkin'?"

The ground along the shore was soft and pliable without distinctive impressions—no recognizable tracks from bear, coyotes, or wolves—just the bloody mess of thrashed soil and sand, cut in deep, wide gashes.

Nickles pointed to a pair of ruts cut deep in the sand and leading straight into the water. "Not unless bears have learned how to do the backstroke in fifty feet of water with a mouthful of venison."

Money's eyes followed the drag marks to the edge of the lake where they disappeared into the deep, dark water. Waves lapped at the shoreline, leaving bloody pink foam along the edge. "Shit."

Nickles stared out over the lake, his hand resting on the butt of his holstered .45, his eyes straining to penetrate the dense fog. He had the thick and muscular build of an outdoorsman, his once black hair overtaken with strands of gray. He kept it cropped short, what the barbers called a flattop. The job had aged him some, slowed his pace a bit, maybe made him a little more cautious and a lot more cynical. He rubbed a callused palm across his cheek and let out a long puff of air. Three weeks ago he'd been sitting at his desk, listening to Travis Tritt, sipping bourbon from a coffee mug and dreaming about retirement. Then the calls started coming in. First it was Mrs. Weingarten's missing collie, followed by a flock of mangled geese in Grant's Cove. And now, this mess.

He knelt down next to the rutted sand and idly flicked a finger through the damp granules. Something jagged and yellow snagged his skin, slicing through the meat of his forefinger. He picked it up and eyed it in the dim afternoon light. A tooth. He turned it over in his hand. It filled his entire palm, extending an inch past his fingertips. He judged it to be over eight inches long, nearly three inches wide and sharp as a straight razor. He turned to Hearld Money, his hand extended, blood still seeping from the gash in his finger. "What the fuck's happening to my lake?"

CHAPTER 2

Deep beneath the blue-green waters of Vivid Valley Lake something vile was lurking around the heavy clumps of weed and thick layers of silt. The thing was once one of God's normal creatures—a gar. It fed on minnows, crayfish and shad and swam the crystal clear water of the Whitewater River. It flourished in the swiftly flowing rapids and basked in deep pools, warmed by the sun. Then, the river was dammed up, the lake was built, the waters deepened and men arrived in noisy machines and sleek boats filled with partiers.

The waters began to sour—run-off from pesticides, industrial waste being dumped in the dead of night and something long-dead rising from the flooded valley floor. The soured water penetrated the gar. The gar was no longer a fish, the feast of the dead had seen to that. Its DNA had a new strand, a twisted strand. Soon, it was becoming something else. Its needle-like teeth grew longer and turned yellow and jagged. Part mutant genetics, part ancient curse, the gar was now a hideous freshwater carnivore, an undead monster that would hunt and stalk and feed.

The monster became aggressive, killing and eating day and night. It never rested. It began to crave bigger prey—warm blooded prey—human prey. As it swam the souring waters of Vivid Valley Lake satisfying its constant craving, it learned there was other prey on which to feast. Buried prey. Dead prey. Cursed prey. And so, the feast began. Soon, the thing would have it all.

CHAPTER 3

Nickles pinched his eyes shut and rubbed his temples. The horns of a vicious migraine were ramming around in his skull and goring the backs of his eyeballs. He fished a pill bottle from his pocket, popped the cap, shook out four long, blue pills and dry-swallowed them. He felt the chalky burn in the back of his throat.

Of all the pains in his ass, Hearld Money was one of the biggest. Money was a 'weekly whiner', calling the DNR hotline whenever someone farted crossways. *Charlie, there's a boatload of drunks and their naked girlfriends tied off at my private dock...Charlie, I got hunters pissing in my sweet corn again...Send Charlie over right away, I got some nosy bastard peepin' in my windows.* With all the corn liquor Hearld Money cooked up in his barn and swilled down his throat, Nickles wondered how the addle-minded old fuck could find his ass with both hands and a topographic map.

As Money's calls became more frequent, so did the ludicrous nature of the complaints. Two weeks ago he'd claimed to have seen a Sasquatch skulking through the woods. Then he upped the ante by weaving a Rod Serling yarn about a silver saucer he'd seen touch down in the hills behind his house. Last week he'd skidded to a stop in front of Nickles' cruiser, hopped out in a drunken huff and demanded Nickles do something about the son-of-a-bitch responsible for stealing and butchering his laying hens. When Nickles asked for evidence, Money handed him a fistful of bloody chicken feathers and a severed hen's head.

Nickles was convinced the old man was slowly going insane, his brain rotting away from all the homemade sour mash he'd strained through a '67 Ford truck radiator and sipped out of a rusty soup can. Shit that vile would have a normal man peeling the skin off his own arms and decapitating himself if he drank enough of it, so Money butchering his own chickens during a session of the blind staggers wasn't out of the question. Nickles had considered strangling the crazy, jake-legged bastard to end the misery, but figured the moonshine would take him soon enough.

The scene spilling out in front of Nickles this time was different. He'd received a radio call from Central Dispatch—Code 10-0—a fatality. The carnage was real, way beyond something a lonely old drunk would stage just so he could cry wolf. Hearld Money's usual backwater bullshit paled in comparison to the mess draped over the log and dragged into the lake. Now Money was a flurry of questions—questions for which Sgt. Charlie Nickles had no answers.

Nickles pocketed the yellow tooth and completed his report, filling out the mounds of paperwork the State of Indiana required of its DNR officers whenever there was an official incident. While the rest of the world had gone digital, Nickles still did everything with ballpoints and carbon paper. Headquarters pissed-and-moaned about his defiance, but did little else, satisfied to scan all his documents into a data base while he rode herd over the growing quagmire in Vivid Valley.

He stowed the papers in his metal file box, climbed back in his boat and fired the engine. As he eased out into open water, he could still hear Money standing on the shore, his feeble frame as fat as a kitchen match, yammering about the bloody mess scattered on the fringes of his property line. Nickles gunned the outboard and sped off. His hand was in his pocket, rubbing the huge, yellow tooth like a spirit stone and praying it would reveal some answers.

Deep below the surface, a rancid, black ooze was mingling with the crystal clear waters of Vivid Valley Lake. The floor of the lake rumbled. A long forgotten tombstone teetered in the sediment and tumbled into a thick layer of festering sludge. It rose into a dense, rolling cloud, pierced by a hulking, black and green body with a ravenous maw full of sharp, yellow teeth.

CHAPTER 4

Mel 'Kingfish' Sharples kept low. His eyes had an icy glare, practiced in the art of subtle deception. He worked by feel—no flashlight, or lantern, or campfire—nothing to give away his position on the shore. He didn't want to risk another run-in with Charlie Nickles and his Department of Natural Resources rule book of fish and game violations. The last thing he needed was a two-bit fish cop sticking his snout into his business. When it came to fresh turtle meat, Kingfish could give a shit less what Nickles' endless book of laws, limits and seasons said. To Kingfish, any season was open season and the weight limit was whatever he could drag in, haul home, cook and eat. He was an aggressive hunter and a master fisherman. That's why they called him 'Kingfish'.

He always set his turtle lines before dawn, baiting the hooks with fresh clumps of beef liver and stringing them around the shallow coves of Vivid Valley Lake. The scent of raw meat lured the turtles off the silt bottom. The barbed hooks did the rest.

Now it was dark. He worked his way around Grant's Cove checking each line. There were twenty-eight in all. With any luck he'd be going home with at least a dozen snappers, maybe more. He used a gentle touch on the lines as he pulled them in. A stray hit could put enough pressure on a turtle line to saw off some fingers if his grip was too tight. He knew a fingerless fisherman wasn't worth a Tinker's fuck to anyone

Tonight, Kingfish had help. Billy Mize was usually too far into his latest meth binge, but Kingfish had caught him during a rare moment of clarity and piled him into his pick-up truck before Billy could back out. Kingfish knew Billy was a sketchy bastard, but when it came to turtlin', he was a master. Billy could snatch a snapper by the tail and yank him off the hook without ever breaking a sweat.

"Sumbitch. Lookit this big motherfucker here!" Billy bellered, holding up a huge snapper by the tail as it bit at the air around his legs.

Kingfish cringed. "Put a cork in it, dumbfuck. You tryin' to get us caught?"

"Sorry, Kingfish, guess I wasn't thinkin'."

"You better start. One more pop from Mr. Law and I'll be doin' some serious time inside."

Billy unhooked the turtle, flung it into a burlap bag and cinched the top shut. "Ain't worth it, not over turtle meat."

"Not over anything," Kingfish grunted.

Billy turned back toward the water. Suddenly he was letting out a stream of high-pitched war whoops that echoed through Grant's Cove like a fire siren.

"Damnit, Billy! Keep. It. Quiet. Can't you get anything through that meth-mushed brain of yours? Now, shut the fuck up!"

Billy didn't shut the fuck up.

"Mize, I gotta tell you one more time, I'm—." Kingfish turned in time to see Billy Mize kicking along the muddy bank next to a tangled bait line. He was pointing at the lake and screeching like an owl. There was a spatter of blood on his cheek and his eyes had gone wild with terror.

Kingfish's eyes darted between Billy's bloody face and the dark surface of the lake. A thick fog was rolling in. He squinted, desperate to get a glimpse of something, anything in the water. "What is it, Billy? Whataya see?"

Nothing but screams.

A barbed fin broke the surface, then a pair of coal black eyes and a gaping mouth. It emerged from the fog like a torpedo and headed straight for Billy. Kingfish rubbed his muddy fists into his eyes, focused, and looked again. The creature's head was now fully exposed. There was a half-eaten snapping turtle lodged in its jaws. The mouth was as wide as a well and lined with rows of sharp yellow teeth.

Kingfish caught a glimpse of its sinister, dead eyes just as it swallowed the turtle carcass and lunged at Billy's thrashing feet. "Shit, Billy, get the hell up outta' there!"

Billy was on his ass, back-peddling through the mud in a frantic struggle to get away. The thrashing failed to give his feet a solid purchase in the slippery bank, pushing him closer to the water and the charging creature. "What the hell is that thing, King?"

"I don't know, but it sure as hell is one ugly, turtle eatin' son-of-a-bitch. Now get your skinny ass up that bank."

"I'm Tryin'."

Kingfish snatched up a dead limb and headed toward Billy. Before he'd taken two steps, the thing had Billy's foot in its jaws and was dragging him into the lake. Kingfish scrabbled down the muddy bank and skidded to a stop just as Billy's head slapped into a rock and disappeared beneath the water. Kingfish waited—one, two, three minutes—for Billy to pop up. Nothing.

When he finally did resurface, Billy was spitting up blood and the creature was still attached. "King...you...it's eating me. You...I...oh Jesus, I..."

The creature thrashed around like a harpooned shark. Billy let out one long burst of painful shrieks. The creature gnawed through his Carhartt jacket, ripping out bits of cloth and bloody flesh. Billy Mize was being eaten alive.

Kingfish was sweating now, sopping it off his forehead with the sleeve of his shirt. He watched in terror as the thing rolled to one side, churning the water and Billy's blood into a crimson froth. Its greasy green and black body broke the surface in a wide arc. Then it pulled Billy under again, his face frozen in horror, mouth gaping and neck gushing thick jets of blood. Kingfish thrust the dead limb into the churning water, desperate to save Billy or kill the beast that was eating him. Billy's hand appeared, making a wild grab for the limb. Then it slipped away and he was gone. As quickly as the attack began, it was over. The water stilled. The lake went calm. Billy and the creature were gone.

Kingfish let the bloody limb slip through his fingers and fall from his shaking hand. As it slipped into the water, the fog began to lift and he was alone in the darkness of Vivid Valley. "Holy shit."

CHAPTER 5

There were no lights on in Hearld Money's house. A single, dim bulb illuminated the barn, casting oblong shadows over hay bales and sacks of grain. A rusty F-150 pickup coasted into the dark barnyard—headlights off, transmission in neutral. The brakes squealed in protest as the truck rolled to a stop by the barn. The driver stepped out.

There was movement inside the barn. A haggard figure scrambled among the shadows. From the darkened doorway came the sound of a shotgun being racked. The driver stopped in his tracks, his hands raised above his head. His voice was a whisper. "Hold up, there, ya twitchy bastard. It's me."

"Me?"came a voice from the darkness. "Don't know nobody named me."

"Cripes, Hearld, what the hell's wrong with you?"

Hearld Money stepped out of the shadows, his shotgun leveled at the driver's face. "That you, Kendall?"

"Hell yes it's me. Put that damn shotgun down, ya crazy imp, before you blow my face off."

Money lowered the shotgun, but stood his ground. "Don't like folks sneakin' up on me, that's all."

Kendall stepped inside the barn. "Yer bein' a bit paranoid, ain'tcha?"

Money spat on the dusty barn floor. "I ain't perry-noid, I'm bein' careful, there's a difference. Now, whatchoo want?"

Kendall watched Money's shaky hands struggling to keep his grip on the shotgun. "Come on, old man, you know what I'm here for."

"You ain't got the law taggin' along behind ya, do ya?"

"Have you gone completely off yer nut? Why'd I do a damn fool thing like that?"

"Suppose you tell me."

"That's crazy talk."

Money rubbed the stock of the shotgun with a dirty palm. "I know for a fact I ain't crazy, but if I was, there'd be a good reason for it. Between the Sheriff and that damned Game Warden, I've nearly been forced to have me a goin'-outta-business sale."

"Game Warden? Ya mean Charlie Nickles?"

"The man never sleeps."

Kendall shook his head. "Yeah, I've heard that said before."

"It ain't right, the way they dog me. I figured once I called in enough shit-silly complaints, they write me off as an old coot."

"How's that workin' for ya?"

A wet, farty noise escaped Money's lips. "Getting' so a man can't earn a solitary dime no more without a shitload of grief. The law's always wantin' to crawl up a man's ass, till ya really need 'em. So, I say, who needs 'em?"

"You can rest easy, ain't no deputies or fish cops been followin' me around. I made sure of that."

"Yeah, well you best not be bullshittin' me. I've heard big ducks fart under water before, so I don't like bein' fed a line."

Kendall leaned against a bale of hay. "Relax, I ain't about to screw up a good thing. Besides, I got the inside track where the Sheriff's concerned."

"Whatchoo sayin'?"

"I'm sayin' the fix is in." Kendall stared at the toe of his boot and kicked a moldy corncob across the barn floor. "And you, and me, and Parker? We golden."

"That ain't much of a comfort. Things tend to change pretty quick in Vivid Valley. And speakin' of the devil, why ain't Parker with you tonight?"

"He's otherwise occupied. I'm doin' this one solo."

Money propped the shotgun against a nearby beam. "You here for the usual, then?"

"I am for a fact." Kendall pulled out a wad of cash and handed it to Hearld Money.

Money ran the bills slowly through his fingers, counting each one as he went. "Yer a little short."

"You what?"

"Yer short."

"Um um, I brung the usual, fur the usual."

Money scratched his armpit and gave his fingers a sniff. "It's gonna be a little higher than usual."

"Bullshit."

"Hey, it can't be helped. Things is tight. It's the economy."

Kendall let out a half-crazed cackle that echoed through the dark, musty barn rafters. "You old prick, Parker said you'd try and pull some shit like this."

"Ain't pullin' no shit. The sad fact of it is, cookin' the finest moonshine in three states is expensive—shellin' and heatin' the corn, purifyin' the water, filterin' the product, maintainin' my equipment—it all adds up."

Kendall walked deep into the darkness of the barn, let out a long sigh and walked back into the light. "Parker ain't gonna like this."

"Don't much care what Parker likes, or don't like, long as he pays fer the privilege."

"So ya wanna be dickish about it, zat it?" Kendall thrust his hand in his pocket and came up with a folding knife. He flicked it open and held it to Money's throat. "We want the usual and we aim to pay the usual price. We good?"

Money eyed the shotgun—close but just out of reach. His hands began to tremor.

"I wouldn't try it bubba. You already got a case of the corn squeezin' shakes. You reach for that shooter and you'll be face down in manure, bleedin' like a stuck pig. It ain't worth it."

"'Spose yer right."

"I *know* I'm right."

Money stuffed the cash in his pocket. "Come on, then, I'll get you yer moon."

Kendall closed the blade on his knife and followed Money to the back of the barn. "That's more like it."

CHAPTER 6

Nickles didn't bother stopping by the Sheriff's Station to report the slaughtered deer. Sheriff Riley would cock his freshly polished, brown cop shoes up on his oak desk, fire up a fresh menthol cigarette, pick at his teeth with a ragged fingernail for a minute, then laugh in Nickles' face. Riley considered him an unwanted necessity in Vivid Valley—nothing more than a fish cop. And Nickles damned sure didn't want Riley, or the media getting their hands on his incident report and turning it into a tabloid headline about *The Vicious Venison Murders of Vivid Valley.* He reached beneath his desk and hit the switch on his document shredder. The six page report went through in a single pass, gobbled up by the whirring steel teeth and sliced into long, ragged strips of confetti.

He took the yellow tooth out of his pocket again, holding it cautiously by the tip. The shape was familiar, but the size was all wrong. He turned to the bookshelf behind him and removed a worn text book. He hadn't opened it in years, not since he'd studied aquatic life at Spencer College to get the Dept. of Natural Resources gig. The pages were worn and dog-eared, filled with the notes and highlights of a bolder, younger Charlie Nickles—notes he'd used to help him memorize the myriad of fish species native to Indiana. He thumbed through the pages. *Sunfish...Bluegill...Catfish...Crappie...* He'd seen that tooth and the fish it belonged to. *Where the hell was it?*

He thumbed past the "D's", page 180, the "E's", page 240. *Where were the "G's"?* He checked again. Page 309, page 311, no page 310. He closed the book and tossed it on the desk. He picked up the tooth again, turning it in his fingers and avoiding the sharp, barbed edges. "What the hell are you?"

CHAPTER 7

Kingfish gathered up his turtle sacks and tossed them up the bank. The burlap writhed and twitched with its heavy load of live turtles. He paced the muddy shoreline where the creature had snatched Billy and took him under. As he walked, he yanked up the heavy metal stakes anchoring the turtle lines and chucked them into the lake, lines-and-all.

Billy's screams had gone on for nearly ten minutes before he went under. Sounds from the lake had been known to carry for miles on a calm night. Kingfish wasn't taking any chances. If someone got nosy and stumbled onto him in the dark, soaked in Billy's blood and carrying gunny sacks full of illegal turtles, things could get ugly.

Kingfish played it out in his head:

"Excuse me, sir, are you injured?"

"No."

"Do you need some help?"

"No, thanks."

"What's in all those burlap sacks you have there?"

"Shit!"

"Oh, my God. Whose blood is that?"

"Double shit!"

Even worse would be expecting anyone to believe what had really happened to Billy in the darkness of Grants Cove:

"Well, we were walking along the shoreline, minding our own, ya know?"

"At seven o'clock at night?"

"Yep, that's right."

"In the dark?"

"Uh, yeah."

"That's all, just walking?"

"Well, sure, we...anyway, like I said we're walking along and all at once this butt ugly, stinkin' monster leaps out of the water, snaps Billy up like a fresh pork chop and drags him off."

Taking a bump for poaching or over-trapping turtles was no picnic, but Kingfish would damn sure do that stretch before he'd let someone toss him in a loony bin for telling mutant monster fish tales. As for Billy Mize, he was a loner. He kept to himself, stealing what he needed to get by and lining his pockets with the money he earned cooking and selling meth. Anyone left on the limbs of the Mize family tree was far removed from Billy, or even more despicable than him. Kingfish doubted anyone would bother looking for him even if they realized he was missing.

Trouble was, with all his bullshit and baggage, Kingfish had actually liked Billy. He did what he was told and he kept his trap shut about what he was doing and who he was doing it with. Kingfish had never wept for a living thing his whole life. Now, staring out into the inky blackness, he felt his eyes begin to well up. He shook his fist toward the bloody water where Billy'd went down. He wasn't through with Grants Cove, not by a long shot. Once he was cleaned up and armed up, he'd be back to kill the thing that had interrupted his turtle hunt and ate Billy Mize.

CHAPTER 8

Gina Vale eased the red and white paddle wheeler away from the dock and steered towards the center of the lake. The last burst of sunlight gleamed off the water, highlighting her chocolate brown eyes and a radiant smile that beamed with generosity. The boat was loaded to capacity and she was energized by the crisp, clean air from surrounding evergreens. Tonight would be a special night. She could feel it. Gina loved the evening shift—those precious hours just before dark

when the setting sun was reflecting off the lake before disappearing in the hills surrounding Vivid Valley. J & K's Tours at Dusk had been popular enough to justify adding a second paddle

wheeler to the fleet. When Gina was asked to pilot the shiny new boat, she nearly squeezed the life out of her supervisor with the hugs and kisses she gave him.

As a supervisor at J & K Tours, Henry Vernon loved to spout his personal work credo: *"Common goals with mutual benefits."* Most of his employees called it troweling out the bullshit. Young, innocent and eager—Gina was sucking it up with a straw. Vernon told her she was enthusiastic, energetic and perky—just what J & K needed for their night cruise crowd.

"Don't consider it just another boat pilot's position," Vernon had told her. "Consider it a new and challenging adventure. Whataya say?"

The compliments made Gina blush. She'd tucked her amber locks behind her ear, gave her lobe a gentle tug and said, "With praise like that, how can I resist? When do I start?"

The evening shift was turning into Gina's dream job. The tours were filled with seniors and couples reminiscing and romancing under the gentle sway of the paddle wheeler as it chugged along around Vivid Valley Lake. Gina was invigorated by her passengers with their affectionate gazes and enthusiastic questions about he history of the lake and Vivid Valley. Best of all, she didn't have to ride herd over crying toddlers, whiny, spoiled brats and snot-nosed, rowdy teenagers.

The last light of day was sliding swiftly behind the hills. The air was heavy with the smell of wood smoke drifting from the campfires at Cedar Bluffs. Gina bumped up the throttle and started the tour, the woman seated directly behind her leaned forward and touched her on the shoulder. "Excuse me, sweetie. May I ask you a question?"

Gina looked at her through the rearview mirror mounted above her boat pilot's chair. She guessed the woman to be seventy, maybe seventy-five. She was tall and slender with snow-white hair and a radiant smile. "Yes ma'am. How can I help?"

The lady pulled at her fingers and gazed out over the lake. "Will we be going near Grant's Cove?"

Gina watched the woman tugging at her arthritic fingers. Grant's Cove was at the far end of the lake—not on J & K's Tours at Dusk itinerary. The trip there and back would put the boats back at the dock well past twilight.

The woman didn't wait for Gina's reply. "You see, Grant's Cove is where I said goodbye to Chester."

Gina smiled, trying to think of a response that wouldn't disappoint. "Was he a boyfriend. Ma'am?"

"Please, call me Ida."

"O'kay, Ida, is Chester an old flame?" Gina was immediately sorry she'd used the word old.

Ida nodded. "I guess you could say that. We were married for fifty-two years."

"My. That's a long time."

A man in the row behind Ida chimed in. "I was married for sixty-three years, myself. What wondrous, glorious years those were. My wife used to tell me, 'Mannie,' my names Manfred, but she always called me Mannie, she'd say, 'Mannie, we're going to live forever.' And I do believe she meant it, too."

Gina throttled the boat back a notch and dodged a chunk of dead driftwood. "How nice."

Ida smiled. "Chester was my everything. I miss him so."

"And he left you at Grant's Cove?" asked Gina.

Ida wiped a tear from her cheek. "Actually, I left him."

Gina scrunched up her face. "Not sure I understand."

"Before the lake, when Grant's Cove was just God's green earth, there was Eternal Peace Cemetery. That's where I said goodbye to my Chester."

"Oh, my."

"Now, don't fret, honey. He's not there anymore, just his memory. They moved Chester and everyone else laid to rest at Eternal Peace before Vivid Valley Lake was built."

"I see."

Ida tugged at her fingers again. "Never quite felt right about that, having a crew of shovel monkeys disturbing all those souls in their eternal slumber."

"It's a violation," piped Mannie. "Not supposed to fiddle with a man's final place of rest."

"I suppose you can't stop progress, though," said Ida.

"Progress be damned," grumbled Mannie. "Men have no right to mess with the natural order of things, especially when it's something sacred."

Gina straightened the paddle wheeler's course and watched the sun sink slowly behind the trees on the far shore. There was a scent of cooked food floating in the air—campers frying up fish, potatoes and beans in heavy cast iron skillets. She sniffed the air and thought about Chester's grave. She never knew there was a cemetery at Grant's Cove. She felt a chilly breeze rush through the window of the boat and scatter a stack of flyers.

"I'd like to go to Grant's Cove just one last time," said Ida.

Gina frowned. "I wish I could, Ida, really I do, but I'm not authorized to take the tour off course and Grant's Cove is pretty far from the docks."

"Come on lady," shouted Mannie over the slapping paddle wheel. "Do it for Ida and Chester."

Others on the boat began to speak up. "We don't mind," said a young couple snuggling in the third row. "We think it's romantic."

"Yeah," shouted someone from the church group in the back of the boat. "Take Ida to see her Chester."

Gina slipped a fingernail between her teeth and bit down hard. Through the rearview mirror she saw Ida's eyes go soft and damp. Soon, cheers were echoing through the boat. *"Chester, Chester, Chester, Chester..."*

Mannie continued to needle. "Please, lady, it's bad enough Ida's had to bury her husband twice. Now she's being denied her final sacred memories? I ask you, is that fair?"

"Well," said Gina, "I'm not supposed to do this, but maybe just this once, in honor of Chester, it won't hurt."

Ida's face brightened. "It would mean the world to me."

Gina pushed the throttle to full speed. The shore was quickly becoming lost in the blues and grays of early nightfall. If she hurried, they could be back to the dock before anyone on shore got antsy and panicked. "Grant's Cove it is!"

CHAPTER 9

A mile from Grant's Cove, deep beneath the surface of the lake, a strong undercurrent began to flow. It picked up silt and swirled it around a long-submerged landform. It was oval in shape and nearly fifty feet in diameter. The soil had been mounded to a height of over seventy-five feet at its peak. Each layer had been packed by hand, one basketful at a time, centuries ago.

The ancient earthen mound rumbled, kicking up sediment and mud. The current carried silt north toward the cove. A second rumble turned the water black. The mound shook violently. The vibrations broke the surface, creating a three foot wave. As the wave broke and headed for the shore, a low growl erupted beneath the water. The earthen mound split open and its protective clay cap fractured. The ancient burial crypt was exposed.

As the mound ruptured, it scattered its contents on the lake floor. Shards of pottery tumbled along in the mud. A hand carved bead drifted along, carried by a black cloud of rolling sediment and sludge. The center of the mound imploded. The surge vomited still more debris into the water, and with it, skeletons. Many of the bones were crushed and broken.

The mound opened further. Full skeletons began to emerge, their jaws gaping, bones fully intact. Three were posed in ritual position, sitting upright. Their arms and legs were crossed and their heads were bowed, just as they had been during their final ceremony—the ceremony of the Mound Builders—the ceremony of the Adena—the ceremony of ancient sacred burial.

The skeletons rose. The skeletons began to dance.

CHAPTER 10

It was nine o'clock when the boat reached the waters over Grant's Cove. Gina was thirty minutes behind schedule. Her supervisor, Henry Vernon, was a nice enough boss, but he was an anal retentive clock-watcher. She knew he wouldn't go into a full-fledged panic for another twenty minutes or so. By then, Ida would be satisfied and they'd be on their way back to the docks at J & K Tours. Gina began cooking up an excuse involving a stalled engine that took longer than expected to get restarted. That wouldn't explain why she'd failed to use her emergency radio to call for help. She'd have to deal with that when it came up—if it came up.

Gina had cut the engine, allowing the boat to drift slowly into the cove. Gentle waves lapped at the hull. There was a chilly breeze kicking up and Gina cupped her hands around her mouth and warmed them with her breath. Fingers of icy wind combed through her auburn hair and tickled down the length of her spine.

Suddenly Mannie stood up in his seat and pointed to a dark patch in the water. "What's that?"

Ida squinted in the direction Mannie was pointing. "I don't see anything."

"There." Mannie shouted, stabbing his finger in the air. "It's right there. Don't you see it?"

Gina scanned the water for any movement. The boat began to rock. "I don't see anything, either."

The young, snuggling couple in the back of the boat continued to neck, ignoring the excitement. A heavy fog began to drift over the cove. A lady from the church group pinched her nose shut and gagged. "Dear Lord, what is that awful smell?"

Mannie was becoming frantic, standing in the isle and bouncing up and down on the balls of his feet. "It's headed right for us. Don't you see it? It's huge."

Gina covered her mouth and nose, trying to ward off the stench drifting over the cove and permeating the chill air. Her radiant smile was losing its luster. The fog was growing thicker, making it impossible to see the shoreline. She turned the key and tried to fire the engine. No luck. She tried again. Nothing.

Suddenly, a terrible scream erupted from somewhere in the back of the boat. The church group was standing on their seats, their faces wide with horror. One of them was staggering toward Gina, her arm drenched in blood, her hand a ragged mess of shredded tissue and bones.

The boat rocked violently, throwing the young, smooching lovers out of their seats. Shrieks filled the boat as Gina continued to grind the starter. Thick, black puffs of smoke rolled out of the engine compartment. The engine coughed, sputtered to life, then died.

"There!" shouted Mannie. "It's right in front of us!"

Then, Gina saw it too—a green and gray mass plowing through the water. Whatever it was, it was moving fast. The water around it bubbled and boiled like a thick, meaty, festering stew. It struck the boat with a glancing blow, puncturing the hull and sending church ladies tumbling into the dark lake. Ida was next, hitting the water with a violent splash. She clawed at the water, screaming for help.

The engine caught, sputtered a beat, then roared to life. "Hang on," Gina shouted. The hull calmed and the boat lurched forward, sending rolling waves of bloody water off the paddle wheel. Ida slipped beneath a wave of blood and disappeared under the surface.

The young couple was untangled and off the floor. They rushed toward Gina, using the seat backs to steady themselves. "Get us outta here. Now!"

"I'm trying," Gina shouted. Her hands began to quake with panic.

Mannie grabbed Gina's arm to steady her. "Do it quick, that thing's coming back."

Gina turned to see where he was looking. There, about thirty feet ahead of them, charging out of the fog, was a monstrous green and gray hulk with coal black eyes. Its manhole-sized mouth was gaping and bloody. Rubbery lips peeled back to reveal hideous yellow teeth—teeth with a human hand lodged between them. Gina felt the boat begin to list to the left as it began to take on water. The engine wavered and died.

Mannie's lips began to quiver. "Wwww…We're sinking. Oh, God…Wwww…We're sinking." Frigid lake water swirled around his wingtip shoes and soaked through his argyle socks.

Gina reached for the emergency radio. She pressed the call button the same instant the creature's mouth crashed through the hull and closed around the meat of her thigh. It tightened the grip on her flesh and dragged her down. The night surrounded them, as hard and dark as a stone wall. It smothered everything but the noisy waves lapping at the rocky shore.

CHAPTER 11

The creature was growing hungry again. It needed to feed. The killing had sapped its strength. The elderly were easy targets. They had put up a minimal fight. Once the boat started sinking they knew their fate was sealed. Two or three well-placed bites and the fight went right out of them. The girl, the one piloting the boat, now she was a fighter. She kicked, she screamed, she punched and she thrashed. After the meat in her thighs was torn out, she thrust a fire extinguisher in its mouth, taking out a row of cracked, yellow teeth. Two quick snaps and it had her arms. As she spewed a thick plume of crimson foam, the creature took her head.

It swam, diving deep below Grant's Cove. There, it found what it needed among the broken, toppled, mossy tombstones. It was an unspeakable porridge of black corpse matter straight from hell. To the creature, it was heaven. It ate, thrusting its head deeply into the graveyard sludge and gobbling it up. Soon, it would be recharged. Then, it would resurface. Then, it would hunt.

CHAPTER 12

Charlie Nickles was still pondering the giant yellow tooth when his phone rang. It startled him and he lost his grip on the tooth. It bounced across the floor, sticking in the hardwood planks. He snatched up the phone and barked into the receiver. "Department of Natural Resources."

"Officer Nickles?"

"Actually, it's Sgt. Nickles."

There was a pause on the line, then a clatter like someone stumbling over a stack of folding metal chairs. "Yes, well, this is Henry Vernon of J & K Tours, over at Vivid Valley Lake."

Nickles waited.

Nothing.

"Mr. Vernon, what can I do for you?"

"Well, I'm not sure. I mean, we have an evening tour out on the lake in one of our new boats and it's late getting back."

Nickles dug a finger into his ear and tried to sound interested. "How late?"

"It was due back an hour ago."

"Where was it headed?"

"It's one of our Tours at Dusk. We started them about a month or so ago, for the calmer set. They've been a huge success for J & K."

Nickles covered the phone, yawned, and continued. "That's nice, Mr. Vernon, now where was the boat headed?"

"Just a quick buzz around the center of the lake, that's all."

"You have radios on those boats, am I right?"

There was a load crack on the line, followed by a clamor of voices in the background shouting questions. "Yes," said Vernon, "we do have radios. The boat pilots are supposed to use them if they have an emergency."

"And you haven't gotten any radio calls?"

"No, and the pilot isn't responding to mine, either."

Nickles stared at the jagged yellow tooth impaled in his office floor. "Have you called Sheriff Riley yet?"

Vernon's voice tightened, growing tense. "The tours are only supposed to last an hour. Gina, the tour boat pilot, is one of our best—very punctual. It's not like her to be this late."

Nickles drummed his fingers on the desk and let out an impatient grunt. "Pid Riley, the County Sheriff, have you called him yet?"

Vernon continued to ramble. "Gina is out in one of our newest paddle wheelers. It's less than a month old. I can't imagine what could be wrong. Why, we've never had a problem like this."

There was static on the line, then rustling noises and something that sounded to Nickles like sobbing. He listened to Vernon's voice on the other end of the phone, rushed and frantic. His emotions were spiraling out of control. "Mr. Vernon, you're not listening. I'm fish and game. You need to call Sheriff Riley, tell him what you've got. He'll take it from there. If he needs my help, he'll let me know."

"Isn't there something you can do? We need someone who knows the lake. There are twenty-seven people on that boat. An accident right now could wreck our reputation."

"Call. The. Sheriff." Nickles didn't wait for a reply, just sat the phone back on the cradle. He felt a migraine returning, dinner forks stabbing away at his eyes as he tried to focus on the yellow tooth. He tugged it out of the plank floor and sat back down in his chair. His mind raced, trying to picture the size of the mouth that would hold such a tooth.

If something that big was in his lake, it would be hard to miss. Even worse, anything sporting a mouthful of hideous, yellow choppers the size of hockey pucks would be hungry. If it became ravenous, something that huge might resort to eating something besides fish—like wildlife, or deer, or anything that moved. Nickles thought about Hearld Money and the remains of the deer, strung out over the log and scattered in the sand. He flipped the tooth end-for-end on the desk, trying to remember the drag marks next to the deer carcass—the length, the depth and the force required to make those deep, thrashing ruts.

He remembered what Henry Vernon had said on the phone. *'We need someone who knows the lake. There are twenty-seven people on that boat.'* He unholstered his .45 and ejected the magazine. Fully loaded. He slapped the magazine back in the receiver and holstered the handgun. Next, he retrieved a Mossberg 500 from the gun rack and loaded it with double-ought buckshot. With twenty spare rounds of double-ought and a box of .45 ammo stowed in a shoulder pack, he was ready to go. He slid on his jacket, shouldered the heavy pack and shotgun and headed out the door.

CHAPTER 13

The ancient mound was now a shambles. Long-dead remains of tribal chiefs and warriors bounced along on swift undercurrents. The earthworks were flattened, scattered along the lake floor in a mixed rubble of artifacts, sludge, mud and bones.

The creature nosed through the remains, its hungry mouth scooping up great piles of rot and decay. Pottery shards and skulls cracked under the pressure of its powerful jaws and yellow teeth. It fed on the sludge of ancient death, consuming the burial site in ravenous gulps. Still more graves began to open. The remains pushed upward, lifting rocks and sand in billowing clouds. And with the clouds, a glowing green ooze. The creature ate. The creature grew.

CHAPTER 14

The sky was overcast, no moon or stars were visible. Nickles kept his boat at full throttle, feeling his way through the pitch-black night. He was wearing a thin, nylon windbreaker and it flapped and fluttered in the breeze as the boat skimmed over the water. The lake was getting choppy, thrashing the boat hull with noisy, wet slaps. A cold spray of lake water soaked Nickles' face and neck. He kept an eye on the eastern shoreline, hoping to catch a glimpse of the brightly lit dock at J & K Tours.

The ragged edges of his migraine were still sawing away at his temples. His hands fumbled for the script in his jacket. He flipped the cap, dumped two Imitrex on his tongue and dry swallowed them. The pain killers had given him a wicked peptic ulcer, or maybe it was Vivid Valley Lake; he wasn't sure anymore.

Vivid Valley was supposed to be his dream gig, at least that's what the brain trust at headquarters had told him—promised him. Promises, promises. Poachers, dopers, jack-lighters, partiers and thugs had turned a dream job into a nightmare. His Post Commander described Vivid Valley Lake as the opportunity of a lifetime. He'd told Nickles it was his chance to finally get a nice-sized slice of the DNR cake. That was a bit of a stretch. Nickles wasn't one to shirk his duties, but each passing day had him salivating over his retirement date with rabid anticipation.

The lake at night time was a wicked deceiver. The most experienced boaters and fishing guides often found themselves disoriented and hopelessly lost once the sun sank behind the tree line. Add a frigid wind, freak snowstorm, a sudden cloudburst, or a heavy blanket of fog and you had a recipe for disaster.

Nickles had once rescued a fishing guide and his two clients in the middle of a blinding rainstorm. Martin Goble, the guide, had

worked the lake from the beginning. Prior to that, he'd owned a
fishing boat on Lake Michigan. Goble had spent more hours on
water than he had on land. On the morning of the rainstorm the
lake was smooth as ice and the sun was in full bloom. Goble left
the public boat launch headed due east. The storm blew in from the
west smothering the lake with wicked bolts of lightning and
deafening claps of thunder. Two foot waves overtook the boat
before they'd hauled in a single fish. Goble managed a single,
frantic distress call before his radio lost signal. Three hours later,
Nickles found Goble and his passengers huddled in the cabin of
the boat, cloaked in a shredded survival blanket, crying like babies.
They were less than a mile from shore. Goble sold his boat a week
later and hadn't been seen in Vivid Valley since.

Nickles marveled at how casual most people were about nature.
Some he chalked up to innocence, some were just plain ignorant.
Why else had so many golfers been struck by lightning during a
thunderstorm trying to squeeze in three extra holes before the
'really heavy stuff' started? And he was still astonished by the
countless, clueless hikers who'd tumbled off a shear rock face or
wandered into a marsh while taking a shortcut through the woods.
He'd learned a long time ago never to thumb his nose at Mother
Nature.

From the inky blackness, a pinprick of light appeared. Nickles
guided the boat towards it, watching it grow larger and brighter.
As he drew closer, the dock lights appeared. One became two, two
became four, until eventually the entire harbor at J & K was
visible. He pushed up the throttle. The boat responded, sending a
heavy wake into the darkness behind the stern.

CHAPTER 15

The creature was getting stronger. When it first smelled the sacred food at the mound, it was ravenous. It feasted, and the feast was succulent, a delicacy of death. It ate its fill, then it slowly died. As it died, a bizarre transformation began to take place. Healthy fins suddenly began to rot. Its body bloated, turning dull green and ash gray. As it continued to mutate, clumps of ulcerated flesh tore from its sides revealing decayed lungs and putrefied organs. The creature's skinny, flat head began to swell. It expanded at an alarming rate, stretching skin and scales into a hulking mass of wretched, quivering meat. The left eye expanded in its socket, turned milky white and popped loose. The creature's gills opened and closed, pulling sacred ooze and silt into every cavity of its dying body.

The thing contorted. It squirmed and thrashed in spastic jerks as the ancient cursed ooze from the burial mound infested its bones and organs. The twitching mouth spewed out clumps of dead gut. The creature rolled from side-to side and twisted in tortured pain. Then, it felt nothing.

Five, ten, fifteen minutes passed. The creature remained in a lifeless lump on the bottom of Vivid Valley Lake. Remnants from its feast swirled around its rotting body, tickling its exposed ribs, washing over its lifeless internal organs and stirring up ancient spirits. The spirits saturated the beast, replacing once-normal fish genes with something cursed and monstrous.

And the curse manifested. The monster moved. The monster grew. It was no longer dead, it was undead. Its mouth changed into a huge, snapping maw full of razor sharp, barbed, yellow teeth. And the teeth grew, protruding from the jaws with loud, cracking noises as they expanded beyond their capacity and stretched the mouth. The lips stretched and made wet, rubbery noises as they peeled back against the force of growing rows of deadly, yellow teeth.

The monster began to swim—slowly at first, then in more rapid, widening circles. Its rotting fins cut jagged swaths through the infected lake water surrounding the mound. The thing relished it, soaking up the ooze seeping from the burial vaults. Ancient death was giving it a second life. It surfaced, and with it a wretched, stench of putrid, undead fish flesh. Scales flaked from its back and floated atop an oily film beside it. The milky, dead eye drooped from the socket, a crushed ping-pong ball of pus. The other eye remained steely and black. It scanned the lake in search of prey. The thing was ravenous again. It needed to feed.

CHAPTER 16

The landing at J & K Tours was a clot of confusion. Employees and patrons were huddled along the dock, talking on cell phones and pointing out at the dark waters of Vivid Valley Lake. Nickles had taken his time crossing the lake, hoping he'd discover the missing tour floating in the darkness with a dead battery, a weary boat pilot and twenty-seven panicked passengers. No such luck.

As his boat appeared from the darkness and cruised up to J & K Tours, people began to cluster along the edge of the dock. They were pointing at Nickles and shouting demands, their frantic requests covering everything from lawsuits to forming official search parties and calling out the National Guard. The crowd parted as Nickles climbed out of his boat and tied off at the end of the dock. A freckle-faced kid shoved his way through the crowd. His fiery red hair jutted out from under a Richmond Roosters baseball cap and he was munching a corn dog while holding a red balloon on a string. He wiped a blob of catsup on his T-shirt and stepped in front of Nickles. "I'll bet it was pirates, huh Mister?"

Nickles paid him no mind.

"That's how pirates do it, ya know? They come up on your blind side and skuttle you and steal your treasure. They usually do it at dusk too." He let out a loud belch and kicked at a dock post with his black high-tops. "If it *was* pirates, they probably killed all the men—just kept the women for later."

Nickles shoved past him and addressed the crowd. "Where's Henry Vernon?"

A scrawny teenager, about five-two, wearing a red and white J & K Tours jacket, his face a riot of acne, pointed to the office building. "In there, I think."

Nickles saw the hysteria in the kid's eyes, probably the most excitement the punk had seen since the local pizza joint had announced free Wi-Fi and drink refills. He walked to the office, ignoring questions from the crowd. When he got inside there was a balding man sitting at a corner desk, wringing his hands and staring out the window at the moonlit water. He was mumbling incoherently and rocking back-and forth in his chair. Nickles approached the front counter and leaned over. "You Henry Vernon?"

The man said nothing, just continued wringing and rocking.

Nickles stepped behind the counter and walked to his desk. "Henry Vernon?"

The man bobbed his head and let out a soft grunt.

"Vernon, did you call the Sheriff?"

"Wh…Who are you?"

"I'm Charlie Nickles. You need to pull it together. Have you called Sheriff Riley?"

Vernon stopped rocking. His eyes remained fixed on some distant point out on the lake. "Right after you hung up…I can't…I called him then…right after."

Nickles crossed his arms over his chest, waiting for Vernon to make eye contact. "And?"

"He's…I…He's on his way, I think."

Vernon was frantic, maybe going into shock. Nickles tried to calm him. "Listen, you're gonna need to get it together. You've got a dock full of people looking for answers. They see you like this and they're gonna flip. You don't want that. I don't want that."

Vernon turned to face Nickles for the first time. "Something bad happened. I can feel it."

Nickles' eyes narrowed. "We don't know that yet. We don't know anything. Now, which way did the tour boat go when it left the dock?"

"Wh…What? It was…where I…"

Nickles grabbed Vernon hard around the neck and pulled his face up close. "You're no good to me like this. Calm the hell down, get a grip and tell me what I need to know."

"What? What do you need?"

"The tour boat, damnit. Which way did it go when it left?"

Vernon's face was now inches from Nickles' chin—pale and pasty, dripping with cold sweat. "North. It was going north and then making a wide circle around the lake."

Nickles felt his stomach roll, as if a striped bass were churning around in his gut on a sea of stomach acid and Imitrex. Grant's Cove was at the north end of the lake. He felt the yellow tooth riding low in his pocket and ran his fingers along the sharp edge. His other hand patted the holstered .45 as he walked out of the J & K office.

"Wait!" shouted Vernon. "Where are you going? Aren't you going to help me?"

Nickles didn't answer.

CHAPTER 17

The darkness around the cove was intense—blackness so thick it was smothering. It enveloped Sheriff Pid Riley and his deputies and swallowed up the glow of their flashlights like a hungry lion. Riley traced the shoreline in front of him, squinting to see anything that looked out of place in the cove. Deputy Dean Hogan followed several paces behind, a maniacal grin on his face as he stumbled over driftwood and rock to keep pace with the Sheriff.

"Englund," the Sheriff shouted, "you see anything?"

Deputy Sherri Englund was straddling a log, fumbling with a willow limb that had snagged her gun belt. "Hard to see anything much, just mud and twigs and rocks, so far." She threw her flashlight beam out over the lake. "The lake looks like a chocolate malt."

"Keep looking, rook."

Deputy Hogan tripped on a clump of thatch and planted a boot in the shallows before regaining his balance. He pulled his sopping boot from the water, cursing under his breath. "Damn, I hate these wild goose chases. Can't see shit out here in this goop."

"Shoulda' brought yer water wings," Riley chuckled.

Hogan stumbled out of the water and raised his middle finger in the inky blackness.

The wind was picking up, bending the tops of elm and cedar trees in the woods surrounding the lake. Riley stepped out onto a sandy wash and stared into the darkness. The icy fingers of a cold breeze blasted down the collar of his uniform shirt. It made the hairs at the back of his neck stand at attention. With the breeze came an overpowering stench. Riley screwed up his face in disgust. He put the wind to his back, fished a cigarette from a pack of menthol 100's and sparked it up.

"What in God's name is that horrible smell?" asked Englund

"You smell it too?" Hogan asked. He wiped his nose on his uniform sleeve and squeaked out a noisy fart. "Nothin' don't get by you, does it Rookie?"

Rookie. Englund couldn't remember when Hogan and Riley had hung that tag on her, but it was getting old. She glanced over her shoulder at Hogan—shirt tail flopping in the wind, hat cocked sideways, uniform pants caked with mud—pitiful. "Yeah," she said, "I smelled it. Kind of a rotten egg stuffed inside a dead rabbit sort-of smell. I thought it was your feet, at first."

Riley took a long drag on his smoke, lit a fresh one off the glowing end, and flipped the butt into the lake. It popped and sizzled as the water smothered the dying ember. "You two wanna cut the shit and get serious?"

Hogan stumbled into the back of Riley and shot him an idiotic grin. "Hey, boss, we gotta keep it light. Am I right?"

"No."

Hogan shrunk back, tugging his muddy pants up over his belly. "Sorry, boss."

"Just keep looking."

They'd been wandering in the dark for nearly an hour when the beam of a halogen searchlight punched through the darkness and bathed them in blue-white light. Riley shielded his eyes. It was coming from the lake. Then he heard the boat motor and spotted Nickles coming in fast and hot. "Heads up. Here comes the fish cop."

"What the hell's he doing here?" asked Hogan.

"Better late than never," Englund mumbled.

"I'd prefer never."

Englund let a slight grin roll across her face. "You say that cause he busts your balls."

"No biggie," said Riley, "This should have been his call-out anyway." He flipped the butt of his cigarette into the water and lit another.

"I just don't like being bested by the hook-line-and-sinker patrol," said Hogan. He pulled off his hat and ran his fingers through his scalp. His thick, black hair looked like his wife had been going at it with a pair of safety scissors again.

"Don't get your colon in a kink. He pins on his badge same as anybody else." Riley blew a smoke ring into the cloudy night sky. "And, for God's sake, keep an eye on the rookie back there. We don't need Englund stepping off into a sink hole or freakin' out and drillin' us in the back with her service weapon."

Hogan gave Englund a slippery smirk. "You heard the man, rookie. Best keep that firearm in the holster, so's it don't go off prematurely."

"And you know about that, too, huh Hogan?"

Riley blew another cloud of smoke, watching Nickles' boat close on their position. "Go easy on the rook, Hogan. I'm trying to mold her into a cop."

Englund's dark, doe eyes went cold, boring a hole in the back of Riley's skull. She ignored the slight. It was a waste of energy. She'd dreamt of being a cop since she was thirteen. She studied law books at the public library, kept up with the latest state and federal regulations, even joined the Junior Officers Program sponsored by her high school. While her friends were out drinking and doping, she was learning firearms safety and weapons tactics. The shooting range and the local gym became her weekly haunts. After graduation she enrolled in the Law Enforcement Program and a college in Jasper. She earned a degree and graduated with honors.

Then came the endless resumes and interviews. The process was bone-numbing insanity. Weeks turned into months and Sherri found herself working a second shift security position at a local scrap yard just to pay off her student loan. The interviews were fruitless. Nobody wanted a rookie. She was about to chuck the whole thing when she got the call from Sheriff Riley.

Riley had met her at the front door of the Sheriff's Station that first day, greeting her with a limp-fish handshake—cold, clammy and damp. "Deputy Englund. Welcome to the law enforcement family at Vivid Valley."

Law enforcement. To Sherri Englund, things had already begun to go sideways. At first, it was simple, the law was the law and her job was enforcing it. Now, that had changed; Sheriff Riley and the Mayor had seen to that. It didn't take Englund long to realize that in Riley's county, law was brokered, bartered and bargained away by slick attorneys, overworked prosecutors and manipulative, demagogging judges. And enforcement? It was administered with a lead-filled sap and a police baton along desolate backroads, usually under cover of darkness. And now, here she was, two years later, stomping around in the dark with the Sheriff and his dickless Deputy, still being called rookie.

"Clap hands," shouted Riley, over the roar of the boat motor. "Here comes Charlie."

CHAPTER 18

The lake had become choppy. Nickles fought for control of the boat while keeping the throttle at full. If the boat tour was near Grant's Cove he'd find out soon enough. If anything else had happened, it could be a long, grueling search. He tried his radio again. Riley and his deputies weren't responding. Either they were ignoring him, or they had run into trouble. Nickles knew, with Riley and his crew it could be either. He'd cleaned up more than one of Riley's botched investigations. He found the Sheriff's work slipshod at best—heavy on computer generated spreadsheets and multi-page reports and short of any factual substance. He gave Riley a wide berth, but was growing weary of his talent for stringing together endless sentences of bullshit designed to do little more than win him another four years behind the badge. Given the opportunity, he'd love to take him down a peg or two.

The radio hissed out a loud burst of static, nothing more. Nickles narrowed his eyes and scanned the shore. Riley and his two deputies were out there, somewhere, stumble-fucking around in the dark. And on the water, stranded or lost, was a tour boat packed with cold and frightened passengers.

There was a light fog forming over the surface of the lake and the sky was black as coal. Nickles bumped up the throttle and tried the radio again. Nothing. He switched on the searchlight mounted on the rail of his boat and scanned the shore around Grant's Cove through his binoculars. If anyone had been there, the rough tide form the choppy lake water had washed away all signs. The tour boat was nowhere in sight. He adjusted the searchlight and focused the binoculars—no passengers in the water and no traces for floating debris. He made one slow circle around the cove, then headed for shore.

Nickles found Sheriff Riley and Deputies Hogan and Englund wandering the cove, ankle deep in sand and muck. Riley was chain-smoking filtered menthols and flicking the butts in the lake while shouting orders to his deputies. Nickles bottomed the boat on a sandy knoll, tied off and confronted Riley. "You practicing radio silence tonight?"

Riley flipped his cigarette into the water and made a sour face. "Nickles, I got no idea what you're squawking about."

"Been trying to raise you on the radio for half an hour. What gives?"

"Beats me, we been right here." Riley fiddled with his radio, twiddling the knobs till a loud squeal erupted and echoed through the cove. "Guess I had the squelch turned down."

Nickles stared at Riley's radio and shook his head. "You manage to stumble across anything out here yet?"

Hogan piped up. "Nothin' but rocks, logs, mud and darkness. Oh, and a gawdawful stink comin' from somewhere."

Nickles sniffed the chill air. The stench was nauseating. Still, deep beneath the overpowering smell of rot, Nickles caught a whiff of something else, something metallic and familiar. Blood.

Riley lit a fresh menthol, inhaled deeply and blew smoke in Nickles' direction. "Probably a bunch of whacked out dopers dumping their trash in the cove."

Deputy Englund held her jacket sleeve over her nose and mouth. "Doesn't smell like any trash I've ever smelled before."

"Why hells bells," said Hogan, "this is turning into a real crime scene. We ought to call this one the 'Great Stinkin' Trash Dump Caper.' We may even have to call out the State Police and the FBI to get a handle on this."

Nickles gave Hogan the fisheye. "Shouldn't you be hunched in a corner somewhere rubbing shit in your hair?"

Sherri Englund let loose a short, nasty laugh. She watched Nickles throw Hogan a badger's grin, waiting to pounce. Hogan started to fire back, but thought better of it.

Nickles gave Sherri a subtle nod. He liked her, felt she had more brains than Riley and Hogan combined. She had a way of plowing through all the crap and getting right to the business end of things—a real pro. To Nickles, she had a cop's intuition. She knew when to talk, she knew when to walk and she could spot a bullshit lie a mile away.

Nickles watched Riley take another deep drag of menthol. "Those things'll kill you."

Riley looked at the smoldering cigarette pinched between his tobacco-stained fingers. He shrugged it off and took another puff. "Gotta die from something."

"You got a handgun on your hip, don't 'cha? Why not just unleash it and eat a bullet?"

Riley flicked the ash off his smoke and cocked an eyebrow. "You're a real ray of sunshine, Nickles, you know that?"

The search continued.

By morning they had walked the entire cove. They had nothing. If the boat had run aground or gotten low on fuel, they'd have spotted it. There was nothing floating on the water and no footprints or personal belongings along the shoreline. Nickles was beginning to think the whole thing was one big goat screw. He was ready to begin focusing the search on the open waters. Then, Deputy Englund shouted something from the far end of the cove.

"Got something over here."

Nickles and Riley trodded along the muddy bank, shoving past Hogan to get to Englund. "What is it?" asked Riley.

Englund held out her hands to reveal a few green, shimmering disks the size of saucers. Fish gills. And something else—stuck in the mud, point up and spotted with blood—a huge yellow tooth.

Nickles felt a bloating bubble forming deep in his gut. Sheriff Riley pulled on a latex glove and lifted the tooth out of the brown muck. "You ever see anything like this?"

Nickles rubbed a dirty palm through his close-cropped hair and shook his head. "Couple days ago."

Riley ran his gloved index finger lightly over the edge of the tooth. His face grew pale and his hands began to tremor. "Sonofabitch."

"Careful," Nickles warned, "that wicked bastard's sharp as a straight razor."

Riley jerked his finger away and eyed the tooth closely. "What the hell we got in this lake that would sport choppers like this."

Nickles stared out over the choppy water, then turned to Riley. "Damned if I know, but I aim to find out." He dug a toe into the muddy bank. His boot caught on something. He lifted his foot, watching a long, thin strand break free of the mud and kick up a pocket of sand. He grasped the end of the strand with his fingers and gave it a tug. With a deep sucking noise, the mud gave up its prize. It skittered along the bank. One end was ragged and the other was double knotted around a barbed hook.

"Whatcha got there?" asked Hogan, biting at his muddy fingernails as he stared over Nickles' shoulder.

Nickles recognized the hook. He'd seen the knot-work before, too. "It's a turtle line."

"Who ya' 'spose it belongs to?"

Nickles fingered the pointy hook, eyeing the knot and the weight of the line. "I got a good idea."

"Think it's got anything to do with this?" asked Riley, holding up the bloodied, yellow tooth.

"Could be," mumbled Nickles. "It could just be." He turned back to the lake. The water was getting calm again. "Whatever happened to that tour boat, we ain't gonna find it stompin' around here in the mud."

Hogan stumbled over a jagged boulder, went down on one knee, then bounced back up. He pulled his hat out of the mud and screwed it back on his head. "Maybe we should get the Navy Seals involved, launch us an all-out assault."

Nickles leaned in close to Sherri Englund. "What that boy needs is a swift kick in the ass."

"Probably enjoy it, too," she whispered.

"Hey now," Hogan yelped. "Leave the rook alone. She's all mine, and she ain't broke in yet. That's my job."

Nickles' eyes focused on a spot deep inside Hogan's skull where a brain ought to be. "Keep it up with the lip, buddy, and I'll shut you down, but quick."

Hogan threw out his chest. It set his double chin into a wag. "Nickles, you got a wild hair up your ass, or somethin'?"

"Fuck with me, you'll find out."

Hogan decided to push it. "You got no call to talk to me like that. I'm an officer of the law, same as you, and I'm here to work."

Nickles hooked a thumb toward Sherri Englund. "Sherri here, she's an officer of the law too. How about showing her a little of the respect you want me to show you."

"Sherri's just a rookie. You know how it is. We have to go hard on her so she can see how a real Sheriff's Deptartment operates. She hasn't got her feet wet yet."

Nickles glared at Hogan's sopping boots and muddy pants. He pointed to the lake. "Look out there, pal. Nothing but millions of gallons of water. Gonna make it hard to turn tail and run away like you did during the infamous Pine Lodge hold-up. You managed to hose that one up good and proper, didn't you? Two innocents gunned down and a pending liability lawsuit against the county— that's one hefty bag of shit to be toting around. A law man, same as me? Not hardly."

Riley threw his hands up in disgust. "You two need to put a lid on it. We still got work to do here."

Nickles grunted. "Best keep your boy on a leash, Riley. You let him roam free, someone's gonna get a serious case of the ass." He watched as Riley's smug face deflated. "This is going nowhere."

Riley spat into the water. "Got that right. Better get started searching the lake, and if I'm not mistaken, that'd be your job."

"You're mistaken. State Police have the closest search and rescue divers. Get them on the horn and fill them in."

The smirk returned to Riley's face. "You tellin' me you ain't diver qualified? How the hell'd you get your fancy fish cop job without bein' fully qualified?"

"Same way you got yours." Nickles twirled the chunk of turtle line in his fingers. "Think you can ride herd on numbnuts and Deputy Englund for a couple hours without getting either of them killed? I got something needs checking."

A sickly grin lingered on his lips. "Where the hell are *you* goin'?"

"There's a little something sticking in my gut that just don't add up."

"Which is?"

"Call it a hunch."

Riley stared at the turtle line dangling from Nickles' hand. His face reddened as he flipped another butt into the lake and lit a fresh smoke. "Don't see why we should take the lead on this one, since it's out on *your* lake, but hell, we got our own boats and a clean line to the State Police. Don't let us interfere with you coffee break."

"You're a Prince, Riley." Nickles started to walk away, then turned back. "One more thing."

"Yeah?"

"Scoop up all those butts before you leave. Don't like 'em fuckin' up my lake."

Rilcy bristled. "If it's your lake, why weren't you called first?"

Nickles turned, took a step closer to Riley, leaned into his face. "Fuck's that suppose to mean?"

Riley shrunk back. "Just sayin…"

Nickles waited for Riley to finish. Nothing. "You wanna police something, police those cigarette butts. It's more your speed." He turned and walked to his boat, fired the engine and blasted out of the cove.

Riley kicked at a stray rock jutting out of the mud. "Damned fish cop." He grabbed a piece of driftwood, using it to drag the cigarette butts close to shore. He didn't see the creature blending with the mud and moss. It watched, waiting for Riley to come closer, waiting for him to stoop, waiting for his plump fingers to touch the water.

CHAPTER 19

Kingfish herded the rusted-out pick-up down the rutted lane that lead to his shack. The thing that ate Billy was still fresh in his mind. He'd pulled in some strange on his lines before—a nest of copperheads, eels, a bloated suicide victim, the Vivid Valley Lake record catfish, even a two-headed snapping turtle once—but nothing came close to the monster that shredded Billy Mize to a pulp and gobbled him up. Kingfish had read about snakeheads and northern pike in an issue of *Avid Angler*, but this? This butt-ugly lump of meat was an angler's nightmare. He was still trying to wipe the image from his memory as it floated around in his scrambled brain—the rancid, rotting flesh, the milky left eye decaying in its socket, all those barbed, yellow teeth ripping away at Billy's insides like a hungry croc taking down an antelope.

He skidded to a stop in front of the welded steel that blocked his driveway. He got out and fumbled for the keys to the double-locked hasp, popped the locks and unhooked the heavy chains. The gate swung free with a rusted groan of protest. He eased the truck trough, leaving the gate open. He wouldn't be there long.

The shack was at the back of a deserted hollow, one of the few remaining strips of isolated land in Vivid Valley that hadn't been swallowed up by the lake. The shack was primitive—no plumbing, no electric, no phone—just the way Kingfish liked it. He parked the truck and entered through the back door. Inside there was a pot of turtle meat he'd left hanging over the fireplace, dangling from an iron hook to keep it warm. He gave the pot a quick stir with a large wooden spoon. The meat had stewed over the coals for nearly twelve hours. The aroma was enticing, but Kingfish had no appetite. He placed the cast iron lid back on the pot and went to the back room. There, he rolled back a dusty scrap of rug to reveal a trap door with a heavy steel ring at the edge. He lit a kerosene lamp and lifted the door on a narrow stairway. The steps were steep and he took them two at a time.

Below, safely stowed in the hand-dug cellar, were the tools of Kingfish's trade—walls lined with fishing gear, traps, supplies, gas powered generators, extra food and fuel, and weapons. His arsenal hung from wall-mounted racks and pegs, loaded and ready for anything he deemed a threat. He raised the wick on the lantern, letting the soft yellow light play on the gleaming hardware.

Billy had put up a vicious struggle against the monster that took him. Kingfish knew this wasn't going to be a catch-and-release critter. This one would be an instant termination, but what to use to get the job done. Kingfish scanned the wall of weapons for the right tools. He made his selections, tossing them on his reloading bench as he went: a Remington 870 Express twelve gauge shotgun, dual Desert Eagle .44's with matching shoulder rigs, and just in case he had to get up-close-and-personal, a fifteen inch machete in a back-mounted scabbard, a SOG Tactical knife with ten inch blade and a SOG Tactical Battle Ax.

He topped off the stack with a case of .44 magnum ammo and one case each of twelve gauge deer slugs and double-ought buckshot. He racked the action on the Remington and ran a palm over the stock. The action was well oiled and smooth. He loaded it with slugs and placed it back on the bench. He was nearly ready.

At the back wall, he opened a hidden panel and removed a heavy, black, triangular-shaped case. He worked the latches, opened the lid and stared at the Holy Grail. It was black, sleek and beautiful. And, most important, it was deadly. Kingfish lifted it from the case, raised it to eye level and sighted it on a silhouette target tacked to the opposite wall. He'd only fired the homemade rig once since he'd built it. That was over ten years ago, but he remembered it like it was last week. He'd taken the rig to the woods, steadied himself in the crotch of an oak tree and drew down on a twelve-point buck. When he squeezed the trigger on the contraption, it launched a sharpened steel rod through the deer with the force of a thundering railroad car. The impact painted the woods with mangled chunks of venison and ruined every bit of edible deer meat. Since then, his homegrown weapon had been stowed in its case collecting dust. Now, he would rely on it to help take down a monster.

He pulled a steel rod from the case, notched it and set the tension to 'full'. "Say ahh, you ugly piece of shit." He squeezed the trigger, unleashing the rod. It left the contraption with a feather-light whoosh, nailing the target dead center before punching through the cellar wall and disappearing in the hard packed earth beyond. He placed the weapon back in the case and packed everything into manageable bundles. The adrenaline from seeing Billy eaten hadn't leveled off. That was good. It gave him a stalker's edge. He was half way up the cellar stairs when he heard the engine. He had company.

CHAPTER 20

Zig ran his fingers through his shaggy purple hair, stretched, and looked out over Vivid Valley Lake. The air was heavy with the scent of pine and the water was smooth as glass. He shaded his eyes from the mid-day sun. "This is it, bro's."

Artie and Juice piled out of the van, a heavy cloud of pot smoke drifting over their heads—a stoner's halo. Juice elbowed Artie, pressing her lips close to his ear. "Ain't exactly paradise, is it?"

"Ah, it'll do, I guess."

Zig pointed toward the van. "Yo, Liv, you gonna join us sometime today?"

There was a rattle of empty cans and bottles, followed by a grunt. Artie put an arm around Juice. "Looks like Liv is partied out before the real party gets started."

Another grunt erupted and an empty tequila bottle bounced out onto the concrete parking lot. "Like hell, I'm just pacing myself." Liv stumbled out, barefoot and bombed. Her coal black hair was a mess and she shielded her bloodshot eyes with a shaky hand.

"Pick up the pace a little, if you can stand it," said Zig. "We keep dickin' around, dudes, and we ain't gonna get a boat."

"Mister enthusiasm," Liv grumbled.

Zig loved Vivid Valley Lake. On any given day, he could be found lounging on the beach or floating along the coves in an inflated truck tube. Today was a special day. He'd pooled enough cash to rent a pontoon and cruise the lake in style. Toss in a shitload of brews in an ice chest, a couple bottles of cheap booze and a baggie of herbal delight and it was party time.

"How's about givin' me a hand with the ice chest, homes?"

Zig stroked his fingers through his beard, the dyed purple ends jutting out in all directions. "Love to, Artie my man, but I gotta go secure our transportation." He dashed off toward the docks, leaving Artie, Juice and Liv to deal with the supplies.

When they got to the harbor, Zig was in a heated conversation with a tall, balding hulk the size of a cement mixer. A weather-beaten sign over the boathouse read: 'Bucky's Beachfront Boat Rentals.' Along the docks, yellow and red posters were tacked on every piling and post. *Party Barge Blowout!! Eighty Bucks Gets You a Full Day on Beautiful Vivid Valley Lake!!*

"Dude," shouted Artie. "It's almost noon already. That's eighty bucks for half a day. Why can't you cut us a break Bucky?"

Bucky shrugged Zig off. "Ain't my fault you can't get up in the morning. Try using an alarm clock."

"That's pretty fuckin' lame, don't you think?"

"You snooze, you lose." Bucky turned to walk back inside. "Makes me no nevermind. I got other renters coming."

"Woah, there, hold up. We need to ice this deal."

Bucky leaned in the doorway, talking over his shoulder. "The price is eighty. You want the boat or not?"

Zig cursed under his breath. "Guess I got no choice, but I ain't likin' your attitude Bucky."

"Ain't sellin' attitude, I'm sellin' boat time, and you just used up another twenty minutes flapping your pierced lips at me."

Zig looked at Artie, Juice and Liv, sitting on the ice chest and shrugged his shoulders. He stuffed his hand in his cut-offs, pulled out a wad of cash and peeled off four twenty-dollar bills. He slapped it in Bucky's callused palm. "Here you go, dude, now which one is ours?"

Bucky pointed to an aging, pastel blue pontoon boat with a broken canopy and dented hull. "That'd be her, right over there."

Artie craned his neck to get a look at the boat. The deck was filthy and there were ragged holes in the carpeting. Spotty mold and mildew stains dotted the torn canopy and the aluminum pontoons were crusted with green and brown lake sludge. "No way."

Zig began to spaz. "Eighty bucks for half a day on that piece of shit. Bro, you have got to be kidding."

Bucky folded his arms over his barrel chest. "I ain't your bro' and I ain't kidding."

Juice's mouth went pouty. She turned toward the lake and lifted the back of her shirt, giving Zig and Bucky a peek at her ass antlers—a pair of angel wings neatly tattooed just above the crack. "Seems a shame not to enjoy such a beautiful day. I mean, a boat's a boat, right?"

"No way," said Zig. "No way I'm shellin' out eighty bucks for that hunk-of-junk."

Bucky handed the money back to Zig. "Suit yourself." He turned and went back in the boathouse.

Zig looked out at the smooth water, then back at the others. He held up a hand and gave them a wink. "Chill for a sec. It's cool. I got this." He went in to talk to Bucky.

Artie stood and lifted the lid on the ice chest, handed Juice a beer and cracked one for himself. "Fuckin' Ziggie."

Juice took a long pull form her beer and kicked out a soft belch. "yeah, fuckin' Ziggie. I mean, he's my boyfriend and all, and he knows how to party, that's for sure, but he has his head so completely buried up his ass sometimes."

Liv rubbed her stinging eyes and yawned. "Just sometimes?"

Artie let out a chuckle that sent beer and foam squirting out his nostrils. "Betcha he flakes and rents that tub," he snorted.

"You're on," said Liv, throwing him a fist bump and finger pull.

"What's the stakes?"

"The huh?"

"The stakes, you know? What are we betting?"

Liv wiggled her eyebrows up and down. "Let's just say they're negotiable."

Artie returned her fist bump. "You're on."

They finished chugging their second beer the same instant Zig came back out of Bucky's office. "We're all set. I just had to wear him down a little."

Liv stared at the ugly blue aluminum monster. "We're takin' it, aren't we?"

Zig waved her off. "It ain't so bad. It floats don't it?"

"'Spose. Remains to be seen."

"Then get the brews and let's go."

"Hold up," Bucky shouted, reappearing in his doorway. There's no drinking on my boats."

Liv flopped back down on the ice chest. "You can't be serious."

Bucky grinned. "My boat, my rules."

Zig started to get in his face, but thought better of it. He ripped one of the flyers off a pole and held it as close to Bucky's face as he dared. "Bucky, man, it's called a party barge. Parrr-Teee. What the hell we suppose to do, play tiddly winks and have a farting contest?"

"Don't much matter to me, long as you don't drink."

Juice let out a long blast of air. "Ain't gonna be much of a party without some drinkage, there Ziggo."

"On the other hand," Bucky continued.

"Oh shit, here we go."

Bucky picked at a scab on his elbow. "I'd be willing to make an exception. For a small fee."

"Bandit," Artie mumbled.

Zig kicked the ice chest. "You're shakin' us down. It's totally not cool."

"Let's not consider it a shakedown. Let' consider it a convenience fee."

Artie shook his head. "How much?"

Bucky scratched his chin and grunted. "I figure forty oughta just about cover it."

Artie palmed sweat from his brow. "Bucky, you're a dick. Zig, pay the man."

Zig pulled the wad of cash back out and peeled off two more twenties. "Got fucked before noon and didn't even get kissed."

Bucky stuffed the cash in his pocket next to the rest of Zig's money and cut a long, loud, stagnant fart. "Keys are in the boat. You all have a wonderful day out on Vivid Valley Lake."

"Fuck you very much," Juice hissed.

CHAPTER 21

Nickles took the last turn at the end of the smooth blacktop highway. Just two miles of gravel road separated the highway from Kingfish's shack. It was little more than a pair of deep, muddy tracks in the earth, winding around boulders, stumps and pot holes. Kingfish kept it that way for a reason. He was a loner who liked privacy and hated authority.

Nickles missed the turn, blowing past the open gate in a shower of muddy pebbles. He'd let his mind wander, thinking of the yellow tooth, the missing J & K Tour boat and the bloody deer carcass. He stomped the brakes, sending muddy gravel over the top of the cruiser and tumbling down the hood. He threw the car in reverse, backed up and scanned the driveway back to Kingfish's. He'd counted on hopping the gate and hoofing it, but the gate was unlocked and standing open.

The front of the shack was visible from the road. The ram shackled roof was a riot of tar paper and asphalt bandages, slapped on to seal out leaks in crumbling, rust-colored shingles. Kingfish's truck was nowhere in sight. Nickles eased through the gate, straddling the ruts to keep the cruiser from bottoming out. He kept a sharp eye on the trees and surrounding landscape. He'd heard about Kingfish's habit of setting camouflaged snares and booby-traps. Rumors had been floated that Kingfish once trapped a trespasser in a staked pit and tossed two dozen hungry snapping turtles on top of him. Nickles could never confirm it, but two weeks after the story made its rounds, Hearld Money showed up at Calley's Café with a riot of bandages on arms, face and neck. When Nickles prodded him for answers, Money said his cat had gotten a little too frisky. Nickles had never seen a cat anywhere on Hearld Money's property or in his house.

He turned the cruiser around in front of the shack so it faced toward the gravel road. If he had problems, or Kingfish started shooting, he wanted to give himself every advantage. He got out, held the door handle up and quietly inched the cruiser door closed. There was a ghostly curl of smoke swirling from the chimney. The shack was dark and quiet. If Kingfish was inside, he wasn't being obvious about it.

Nickles walked quietly to the north side of the shack and peered around the corner. His shoulders slumped and his mouth dropped open as he took in the scene laid out in front of him. There were hundreds of dark brown and tan turtle shells littering the landscape. Some were dried, lacquered and mounted on the outside of the shack; others were hung on stakes and poles to dry in the sun. Off to the left, he spotted a row of fresh kills, the shells still heavy with clumps of mud and thick layers of green moss. The shells had been picked clean of meat, the snappers separated from their ancient armor. In a long galvanized tub, Nickles found stacks of preserved turtle heads and claws. He crept closer to the shack, watching the ground for trip wires and snares. Two freshly butchered turtle shells were propped against a rusty steel drum, turtle blood still draining into the damp ground. The shells showed huge bit marks, the signs of a fierce battle with something vicious and powerful, but what?

Nickles inspected the shells closely, placing his thumb in one of the bite marks. There was room enough for a second thumb in the unfilled gap. He pulled the yellow tooth from his pocket and placed it in the bite mark. The fit was perfect.

Kingfish's truck was parked between two aging walnut trees behind the shack. There was no sign of his boat. Nickles wondered if he was still out on the lake and what kind of righteous shitstorm would develop if he came up against Sheriff Riley and his idiot deputy. Hogan would be clueless, far too ignorant to realize the danger he was in. Nickles didn't want to think about it. He crept over to the pick-up truck, placed his hand on the hood. Warm.

There was a heavy chest freezer on the back stoop with a cord running to a gas generator. The generator was fueled-up and running. He lifted the freezer lid. It was loaded to the top, full of packages tightly wrapped in butcher's paper. Each bundle was marked in sloppy block lettering with an ink marker. **'TUrTle MeAT'**. He closed the freezer and tried the back door. The knob turned. It was unlocked. He slowly eased the door open.

Inside, he found himself in total darkness. He pulled the Maglite from his belt and switched it on. As the flashlight beam played along the walls and floor he caught glimpses of dried snake skins, animal hides, deer antlers, a string of raccoon tails and stacks of beaver pelts. They were tacked, hung and mounted on every square inch of flat space available. There were shelves along one wall, stocked with canning jars full of turtle meat and pickled turtle eggs. A five gallon vat filled with green liquid and floating blobs of greasy, brown flesh was sitting in the corner. It gave off a noxious stench that reminded Nickles of a batch of Hearld Money's lye soap, cooking away in the belly of one of his burned-out moonshine stills.

He diverted the flashlight away from the vat and started to back out of the room. Then, he spotted it, on the edge of a small wooden table. The tooth. It was smaller, not as jagged or yellow, but it was the same shape. And on another shelf behind the table, a glass jar full of them. He lifted the jar, turned it in his hands, shook it and tilted it closer to the light. The teeth clinked against the glass and clanked on the metal, screw-top lid. He put the jar down and felt a puff of air on the back of his neck.

He heard Kingfish before he saw him.

"Got a warrant?"

Nickles turned to face him—scraggly hair and beard, an icy stare and lips that gave up little more than a smirk. He was standing in a darkened doorway, his hair and beard a wiry brush pile of muddy brown. He was wearing a sleeveless, tie-dyed shirt and moss-green cargo pants that had worn thin at the knees. His eyes, cool and calculating, shifted between Nickles' sidearm and the glass jar of teeth.

"Gate out front was open, so I came in."

Kingfish folded his arms and let out a feral growl. "Just cause my gate's open, don't mean the welcome mat's out."

Nickles picked up a turtle shell, ran his fingers over the deep ridges in it, and hung it back on the wall. "Wanted to have a look around, maybe talk awhile."

Kingfish walked to the turtle shell Nickles had been handling and straightened it on its hook. "You forget how to knock?"

"Nope."

"Did you knock?"

"Nope."

"You got a warrant?"

"Wasn't figuring on needing one."

"You figured wrong."

Nickles pulled the raveled piece of turtle line from his pocket and held it up in front of Kingfish. "Looks like your handy work."

"Prove it."

"I recognize the knot. It's your style, right?"

"It's just a friggin' knot. Lots of folks tie that kind."

Nickles gave Kingfish a look of doubt, allowing the hint of a grin to form on his lips. "Ah, but not the official Mel Sharples, Kingfish style, double-drawn, turtle knot."

"You blowin' smoke up my ass?"

"Wouldn't dream of it." Nickles twirled the line between his thumb and forefinger and watched the frayed end unravel around the hard, tight ball of the knot. "You been to Grant's Cove lately?"

Kingfish diverted his eyes from the turtle line and stared into the floor. "There some law against bein' in Grant's Cove?"

Nickles gave the line a tug, admiring the integrity of the knotwork. "Nope, not unless someone was trapping turtles over the state limit, or maybe catching something more than they bargained for."

Kingfish let his left hand drift to his side. There was a snub nosed .38 in the small of his back, concealed behind a cloak of rainbow tie-dye. He'd managed to grab it, tuck it under his shirt and concealed the trap door to his cellar just as Nickles boot heels had cleared the threshold of his back door. He didn't want to pop Nickles, but if the shit got deep he'd do what he had to do.

Nickles was no stranger to gunplay. He'd had a piece pulled on him before. Having a gun in his face always gave him that dizzying feeling of gut-wrenching nausea in his belly as the adrenaline surge kicked in. He was getting that feeling now. His .45 was loaded and ready, but still holstered. As he slowly reached for the grip, his radio went off. He kept an eye on Kingfish, dipping in and out of the darkened doorway as he keyed the mic on his shoulder unit. It was Central Dispatch requesting he call the Mayor ASAP. He questioned the dispatcher, who knew little more than the basics. *'Urgent request from the Mayor Smythe involving an emergency of unknown origin at Vivid Valley Lake. Respond immediately.'*

Nickles signed off and dialed the Mayor on his cell. He kept his left hand on the butt of the .45 and both eyes on Kingfish. Mayor Smythe answered on the second ring. His voice was strained, the tone frantic. "Charlie? Charlie Nickles, are you there?"

"I'm here."

"We got problems. I need you in my office."

Nickles rubbed his brow, keeping an eye on Kingfish's hands. "Kind of tied up right now. It'll have to wait." He could hear shouting in the background, chirping through the cell phone in delayed garbles and a rush of static.

"You'd better get untied, Charlie. Now."

Nickles protested. "Can't do it. I'm in the middle of something."

"Oh, but you can. This is an emergency."

Emergency. Mayor Smythe used the word on Nickles like it was a magical pass key, mystically hardwired directly to his brain. *A back-up at the boat launch? Emergency. A fisherman with a flooded outboard motor? Emergency. No diet sodas and sugar-free snacks in the Pine Lodge vending machines? Emergency.*

Nickles watched Kingfish as he faded back a step. His hand was now drifting to his hip, his fingers drumming on the waistband of his cargo pants. "Soonest I can get there is about an hour." He had his hand on the OFF button, ready to end the call and deal with Kingfish.

"They're gone, Charlie, all of them."

"Wait, what?" Who's gone?"

"All of them—Sheriff Riley, his deputies, they're gone."

Nickles stared at the cell phone, expecting Mayor Smythe to squirt out of the speaker and leak all over the floor. "Whataya mean, gone?"

"Just get down here!"

The signal went dead.

Nickles flipped the phone closed and pointed a finger at Kingfish. "We aren't through yet."

Kingfish kept his fingers on his waistband. "You arrestin' me?"

Nickles was already on his way out the door. "Just stay put."

"So it's *house arrest*, then?"

"I'll get back to you once I put a few fires out."

Kingfish let his hand drop and burst into a fit of laughter. "Well I'll be damned. I knew you was some kind of top-notch Game Warden here in the Viv. Didn't know you was a fireman too. You truly are a Jack-of-all-trades. Oh, wait, that's Chuck-of-all-trades."

Nickles kept walking. "You just be here when I come back."

"Why, hell yes," Kingfish shouted after him. "No problem. Ain't like I got a life or anything. Do me a favor though, Game Warden, knock next time, else I might not be as cordial."

CHAPTER 22

Zig was at the helm, cranking the motor before Artie and Juice had the ice chest loaded. Liv had managed to find a strip of shade under the broken canopy. She flopped down and waited for Juice to crack another beer and pass it over. Zig gave the engine a few more cranks. It finally caught, belching and sputtering black clouds of exhaust smoke.

"No problem, guys." He goosed the throttle. The engine choked, then idled-up. "Just need to blow the 'ol cobwebs outta this puppy, that's all."

Juice opened a beer, hopped back on the dock and waved her arms in a wide arc. "Not so fast. A fine watercraft like this can't cast-off without a proper christening, can it?" She held the bottle of beer at hip level and cocked it back like a Louisville Slugger. "I dub thee the S.S. Shitheap." The swing connected with the aluminum pontoon, sending glass and foam over the deck and into the water.

Artie let out a beer belch. "Sonofabitch, it didn't sink." He held a hand out to Juice. "Come aboard, me lady."

Juice hopped on as Zig punched the throttle and sent the boat out of the harbor in a choking plume of black exhaust and raw fuel. Artie hung on the rail while Juice staggered her way up to the helm. She slipped an arm around Zig and nibbled at his ear lobe. "So, Captain," she cooed, "where's this cruise headed?"

Zig steered the S.S. Shitheap out of the harbor and headed north. "Party City, baby. Party City."

Artie plopped down next to Liv and sipped on his beer. He soaked up the sun, letting the wind whip through his long, straight hair. The boat plowed through the water like a coal barge, kicking water off the bow in gushes. The engine continued to cough and sputter and the boat rocked up and down like a carnival ride. Zig dicked with the throttle, cranking it up and down in an attempt to smooth things out. Liv got up and stumbled to the back of the boat. She kept a white knuckled grip on the rail while barfing into the lake.

"Whoa, she's partied-out, dudes." Zig was dancing around like a circus monkey, laughing and pointing at Liv's tossed cookies floating behind the boat. "Technicolor yawn, baby."

"Up yours, pal. I wanted to ride a teacup ride, I'd go to a fuckin' county fair. This ain't relaxing and it ain't fun."

Artie scooted into Liv's shady spot and popped another beer. "This heap is doin' like zero naughts, Zig. You sure we ain't draggin' the anchor?"

"Or the dock?" Liv added.

Zig tossed his hands in the air. "Come on, guys, don't think of it as a beat-up old boat; think of it as a twenty-four foot, seventy horsepower, well-worn party barge."

"Yeah," said Liv. "A rotting, under-powered, powder blue, hundred dollar, pathetic party barge."

Artie corrected her. "That's a hundred and forty dollar, pathetic party barge."

Liv ran the toe of her sandal over a crusted barf spot on the carpeted deck—a relic from past partiers. "Did I forget to add gross and disgusting?"

"You guys worry way too much. Just relax and leave it to the 'ol Zigmeister. We're almost there."

"Almost where?" asked Artie.

Zig pointed to a cove up ahead. "There. It's secluded, it's private and the water's great for a swim." He steered the S.S. Shitheap toward Grant's Cove. "It's perfection."

"Purrrrrr-fection," Juice purred into his ear.

Liv heaved another load into the water and wiped her chin with the back of her hand. "Whatever, as long as we stop soon, this high-seas roller coaster ride is killin' me."

Zig spud-chugged a bottle of beer and tossed the empty into the waves. "You just don't have yer sea legs yet, but yer in luck." He tugged a clear plastic bag full of herb from his back pocket. "I got something that'll fix you right up."

Liv wrinkled her nose and pinched her eyes shut. "I'll pass."

"Dude, this stuff is primo. It's great for nausea."

Liv waved him off and plopped back down next to Artie. When it came to pot, she was a lightweight. She'd tried it a few times, but nothing like Zig or Juice, who seemed to be lit-up most of the time. She never got the kick. In fact, it made her sick and screwed with her balance. And then, there were the migraines—skull-splitting, ear drum piercing, eye swelling migraines—the type that crippled her for days and forced her to avoid bright light as if she were one of the mole people. She didn't see the point.

"Suit yourself," Zig shouted. He fished a pack of rolling papers out of his other pocket and began building one of his famous mega-joints. By the time the boat drifted into Grant's Cove he had the first one sparked-up and three others staged and ready. He turned to Juice. "Drop anchor, Sweet Lady J."

"Aye-aye, Captain."

Zig tugged an inner tube to the front rail and lowered it into the cool, calm lake. "Last one in's a scum-sucking shit eater." He eased into the tube and paddled out into open water.

Artie elbowed Liv. "A regular Diver Dan, ain't he?"

"He looks like a dick in a donut."

Artie coughed out a mouthful of beer, shooting thick, snotty foam out his nose.

Zig eased back in the inner tube, plucked a joint from behind his ear and a lighter from his sopping shirt pocket. "This is the life." He fired up the joint and took a killer hit. He held it in, letting the smoke and sensation build in his brain. *A thousand one, a thousand two, a thousand three, a thousand four and release.* He blasted the smoke out in a massive, coughing cloud. "Yowzah wowzah."

Juice was rustling around in the ice chest and came up with a chilled bottle of tequila. She held the frosty glass to her cheek, then uncapped the bottle and took a long pull. Her head and shoulders shook violently as she pulled a sour face. "Shit, that's good stuff." She tipped the bottle and took another blast. "Good, good stuff."

Liv looked at Artie, vomit slobbers still clinging to her chin. "She's gonna pay for that later."

"Um Hum."

Juice downed another mouthful and capped the bottle. She tossed back her fire engine red hair, reached behind her back, unhooked her bikini top and let it fall free. She cupped her breasts and let out a whoop, "Let's get this party started." She staggered back to the helm, found a boom box and dialed the volume up to nine. "Yeah."

"So much for a nice, quiet, relaxing cruise around the lake," Artie grumbled.

Liv let out a laugh that sounded more like a squeak. "You should know by now, Zig don't do anything quiet."

"Or relaxing."

Juice was beginning to feel the tequila kicking in. She wiggled her ass and did a quick one-eighty spin before shucking her bikini bottoms and diving into the lake. The water was clear and cold, but had a funny odor. She couldn't quite place it—sulfur, lye, maybe sewage. It burned her nose and made her skin itch.

"Baby, you are a knockout," Zig shouted. "I could so do you right now."

She swam over to him, plucked the joint from his fingers and took a long, deep hit.

"That's the stuff dreams are made of."

She coughed out a cloud. "A bit harsh, though. Not up to your usual standards, bro. Where'd you score it?"

"Beggars can't be choosers, sweets."

Juice took another toke. "Just sayin'."

Zig pinched the joint between his fingers and inhaled. "You gotta wait for it to kick in."

Juice scratched at her arms. Her skin felt hot and oily. "I gotta get out for a bit. Feels like there are ten thousand termites wriggling around under my skin."

Zig spun the tube around in the water to get a better look. He saw the strain on her face, like she was about to burst with something. "Come here, babe, you just got goose bumps. I'll rub 'em out for ya.'" He kicked his legs, using his feet to duck-paddle towards Juices' naked breasts. She bounced up and down in the water like a fishing bobber.

Below the surface, the creature watched. A toe brushed its milky, dead eye. Another skimmed the top of its head. Its jaws slowly hinged open. The creature sensed the movement above, spotted something stirring in the water. It hungered. It waited.

Zig floated closer to Juice and wrapped his legs around her waist. She gave him a peck on the cheek, then kissed him deeply. "Babe, I'm gettin' some major league wood here. You do know that right?"

She scratched at a red spot on her shoulder next to her new rose tattoo. "You've always got major league wood."

"True dat."

Juice began to giggle, then stiffened in the water as if she'd been shot in the back. Her eyes went wide and her wordless mouth flopped open.

"Juice? You o'kay?"

She yelped as a set of razor sharp, yellow teeth slammed into her. The creature rose and bit at her back, legs and neck. The first solid chomp took out the tattoo; the second tore through her wind pipe.

Zig fell back in the inner tube, screaming in high-pitched wails and paddling with his hands. "Holy shit, get this thing off her. It's killing her. Help!"

Artie remained where he was, eyes closed, assuming it was another of Zig's sick jokes. "Yeah, yeah, we hear ya' there Zig. It's a man eating shark, we're all gonna die. Yadda, yadda, yadda."

The creature's head broke the surface, followed by a rancid smell of rot and sulfur. Its lips parted and pulled upward as the hideous mouth opened wide to finish Juice off. She was powerless to scream. Her arms flailed in the water as she swatted at the thing's gaping maw. She coughed lake water and a black glob of blood.

Zig continued paddling and screaming, trying to guide the inner tube toward Artie, Liv and the boat. "What the hell are you, you ugly, stinkin' pile of shit?"

The creature continued to feed on Juice's body. Blood was now gushing from the stump where her head use to be. Her arms beat aimlessly at the water. Her meatless legs hung limp and lifeless, just below the bloody surface.

Zig had reached the boat and was clawing along a pontoon, desperate to reach the ladder. Artie and Liv were up now, Artie scanning the bloody water where Juice had been attacked. "What the hell happened out there?"

Zig began babbling. "Fuckin' thing is huge. Thirty feet...dead white eye...wicked yellow teeth...eating Juice's head..."

"Shit, Liv I think he's finally cooked his brain."

"He's fried, dried and laid to the side."

Then Artie spotted something in the water. "Ah, I don't think so. Look."

Liv squinted where Artie was pointing. She caught sight of the thing just as it darted toward the inner tube. Zig felt sharp pains shooting through his legs. "Oh, God, it's eating me. Help me. Please, God, help me."

Each new bite made Zig shriek in agony, jerking and thrashing to keep his grip on the ladder. Yellow teeth gashed his shins and ankles. His mouth drooped open in a silent, slobbery scream. His eyes fluttered, going solid white as they rolled back in his head. The stench of death rose from the water and rolled around his tortured face.

Artie stared at the creature's deformed head—the green and gray skin sloughing off like mildewed wallpaper, the milky dead eye dangling loose in its exploded socket, bloated and blind. It flicked its disfigured tail and whipped the bloody water into a thick, pink froth.

"Oh God...Sweet Mary..." Artie was giving in to the shock of witnessing the slaughter, his high-pitched shouts clashing with Zig's painful screams. "What's happening? Liv, what's happening? Please, tell me what's happening?"

Zig made one last grab for the ladder and pulled himself up. Then it hit. The creature pulled him down, dragging his torn-up body through the inner tube like thread passing through the eye of a needle. His mouth made wet smacking sounds, struggling to form words. Zig and the creature disappeared beneath the bloody foam, deep down, where the water dimmed to a coal black, deadly murk.

Artie crab-walked away from the ladder. "It's...I think...It's gone...gone..."

Liv peeped over the edge of the S.S. Shitheap, watching the ladder twist and jerk in the water. "Maybe not."

"No…No…We…We're safe now…Pretty sure we're safe…"

Liv squinted and looked again. It was coming back. Whatever it was, it wasn't going to eat and run. It shot alongside the boat and she snatched a beer bottle and took a wild swing. It connected with the dead eye and shattered into jagged, brown shards. Liv reached for another bottle, but the boat rocked violently, tossing her into the lake.

The thing was on her now and going berserk. It locked its jaws around her rib cage and punctured her lungs. Her face was smeared with blood, her eyes filled with fear. A final blast of air bubbled through her lips. Her eyes slammed shut. She could smell rotted fish—and something else—her Mother's freshly baked bread.

A huge geyser of red water gushed over the deck of the boat and showered chunks of Liv's torso in bloody clumps around Artie's feet. The water calmed. There were no more screams. The creature was gone. Artie was alone. Sweat and tears were pouring down his cheeks and chin. His heart was racing as he tried to make sense of it all—the blood, the howling, the violent thrashing, the carnage and the hideous thing in the lake. *Where had it come from? What the hell was it? Why was it eating his friends?*

He wanted to go home.

CHAPTER 23

Nickles didn't need another one-on-one with Mayor Curtis J. Smythe. What he really needed was a fistful of Ibuprofen and a long nap. The gears in his head were turning, but exhaustion was shearing off the teeth. He needed answers. Where did the yellow tooth come from? Why did Kingfish have a jarful of smaller ones and where had he gotten them? What else was he up to? What had happened to the J & K Tour boat and its passengers? And what the hell created that horrifying stink-of-a mess Hearld Money had stumbled onto? The questions flopped and wallowed around in his brain like a pregnant carp in shallow water. The answers would have to wait.

Smythe had told Nickles to meet him at his office. Nickles knew that when Mayor Smythe said office, what he really meant was his favorite watering hole. For as long as he'd been putting up with Smythe's bureaucratic antics he'd never once set foot in the mayor's real office.

Nickles walked in the back door of The Golden Anchor, letting his eyes adjust to the dim light and smoky air. Smythe was at his usual table, a tumbler of scotch in his hand and a smoldering cheroot resting in a heavy glass ashtray. He was firing down gulps of scotch and yapping on his cell phone. When he spotted Nickles he waved him over and slapped the cell phone shut.

"Where've you been?"

Nickles gave Smythe the hard eye, watching his fat fingers pick up the cigar and roll it between his lips as he puffed it till the tip was cherry red. "Got a bulletin for you, I'm busy. Deal with it."

Smythe bunched his cheeks and blew out a cloud of angry smoke. At sixty-six he was marshmallow soft and eighty-five pounds overweight. That didn't stop him from trying to be an arrogant, sadistic taskmaster. "I don't like to be kept waiting. I've made that quite clear."

Nickles waited for Smythe to down the last of his scotch and order-up a fresh one. "Looks to me like you found something to pass the time."

"Better sit down. You're gonna need a couple belts too, before we're through."

"I'll pass." Nickles sat down across from Smythe. "So, what's the bug up your keester this time?"

Smythe blew a thick stream of blue smoke at Nickles and put the cigar back in the ashtray. "Don't you smartass me. We got a problem."

Nickles eyed the gin blossoms streaking across Smythe's nose and cheeks. The scotch had them in full bloom. He knew the mayor's routine—up at seven to start his day with five or six brewskies before bumping it up a notch with a couple Kentucky bourbon shooters—it was his daily ritual. Any serious business with the mayor had to be conducted by noon, after that he was headlong into the hard stuff. Nickles checked his watch. It was 3 P.M.

He ordered coffee, black and waited for it to come. He blew the rim of the mug and took a sip. "Whataya mean we got a problem?"

"Surely I don't need to refresh your memory. You've been to J & K. You know the tour boat is missing. Now we've lost contact with Riley and his deputies. People are getting frantic. We don't need that, not in Vivid Valley. And just as surely as a big brown bear takes a dump in the woods, there'll be lawsuits. I don't need to tell you how devastating litigation can be. Hell everybody with two dimes to rub together and a blister on their ass is looking to sue these days."

Nickles sipped his coffee, felt the bitter brew kick around in his empty stomach. He pushed the cup away and folded his hands in front of him. "You keep saying we. Why you insist on wrapping me up in all this?"

"Aren't you listening to me? Sheriff Riley? His deputies? They're MIA—no response to radio calls, no sign of their boats, nobody back at the Sheriffs's Station— nothing."

Nickles took a deep breath and let it out slow and loud. "Riley. Mr. By-the-Book. The guy's a total pain in the ass. Wouldn't surprise me if he caught his deputies violating some obscure subsection of his thousand page rule book. Probably got up at state headquarters drumming them out of the unit right now."

"So this is some big joke to you? You think cause you and Riley lock horns that makes him insignificant? And let's say he is at headquarters, that doesn't explain the unanswered calls and the missing boats."

Nickles threw up his hands. His face began to redden. "So what are we supposed to do?"

"Simple," said Smythe, "the community depends on that lake— for their entertainment, their recreation, for income—which means they depend on you."

"Don't," Nickles growled. "Don't you back a truckload of shit like that up and dump it in my lap."

"You're not hearing me. When that lake is humming, the community is humming. When things are humming, that means cash registers are ringing and people are happy. This valley needs that happy, and all the money that goes with it."

Nickles stared out the window, watching the clot of people and boats out on the lake, each one eager to find their little chunk of temporary joy while Mayor Smythe and the Chamber of Commerce dreamed up new ways to exploit them. Nickles longed for the days before Vivid Valley had been turned into one of Indiana's largest government funded swimming holes. Back then, he had freedom and authority. He had a job where he could make a real difference. He was his own boss and rarely saw a supervisor. He came to work early and stayed well past midnight. He was proud of his badge and all that it stood for. After news of the lake came to Vivid Valley, things began to change. Politics played a big role in every aspect of the community. Once politicians sunk their greedy hooks into things, logic and legality went out with the tide. Soon Nickles was ass-deep in paperwork and pencil pushers. He had supervisors up his ass on a weekly basis and every federal agency with more than two letters in their acronym was crawling over Vivid Valley burning up tax dollars at light speed. Then the money got tight and big men in tailored suits started visiting

Nickles and asking him to do things—things he should've refused to do.

Nickles watched a punk on a jet ski take a hard dump in the wake behind a cabin cruiser before turning back to Smythe. "You didn't ask my opinion yet, mayor, but since we have a problem we have to deal with, I'm giving it to you." He pointed out the window at the crowded lake. "This valley was a better place before that damned lake out there came along."

Smythe gulped a mouthful of scotch and slammed the tumbler on the table. "Don't bitch, Charlie, it pays your salary."

"Everything's about money with you, isn't it mayor?"

"It's the way of the world."

"Not my world." Nickles got up to leave.

Smythe adjusted his tie and checked his Rolex, as if he had someplace else to be. He ordered another scotch and stared over Nickles shoulder at the busy lake. "Look, Charlie, you don't think it bothers me what's under all that water out there?"

Nickles watched Smythe fidget, waiting on his refill. "Yeah, I can see it's got you all bound up."

"Just remember, Charlie Nickles, you weren't exactly innocent, or blameless in that whole mess. Can you say willing participant?"

Nickles sat back down and slammed his fist in the table. The impact made Smythe jump. "Alright, you wanna talk we? Let's talk about what we should have done years ago. Let's talk about what we sacrificed to get that giant kiddie pool out there. Let's talk about how we ignored the living and the dead and watched them be violated. And—here's the biggie—let's make sure we report what we should've never let happen in the first place. We owe it to those people and their families."

Smythe's crimson face turned a deeper red. His jaw tightened and began to bunch. He picked up his fresh drink, but his hands shook so badly he was unable to drink. He set the tumbler down, leaned in and took a noisy slurp before regarding Nickles. "Charlie, be reasonable. You know that's not going to happen."

"Maybe you need to consider someone besides your pool of faithful voters, Mr. Mayor."

"It goes deeper than that."

Nickles glanced back at the lake and began to laugh. "Yeah, at least ninety-five feet."

Smythe placed his chubby hands in his lap, unable to control the shaking. "Those plots, the cover-up, I don't think you realize the damage that would be done if anyone knew what was left down there."

"I don't think you realize the damage that's already been done." Nickles got back up. "Just you remember, nothing stays secret forever."

Smythe grabbed his arm. "We aren't through yet."

Nickles jerked away. "I say we are." He headed for the door.

Smythe shouted after him. "Sheriff Riley and his deputies are missing. You're the only law left now.".

CHAPTER 24

Nickles knew Mayor Smythe had shed his share of the guilt long ago. Money does that to people. Nickles couldn't put his conscience on ice that easily. It bugged him, tugging him out of a sound sleep at night. He couldn't shake the image of the cemeteries—all those abandoned souls—sacred graves being left behind—flooded with millions of gallons of water. And for what? To save money and keep construction of Vivid Valley Lake on schedule and within budget. So the graves were never relocated, as originally agreed.

When families began showing up, curious about the fate of their loved ones, they were shown wooden dummy boxes marked: 'BURIAL REMAINS', along with weather-tight burial vaults and lovely new coffins, all courtesy of Uncle Sam. The thing was, none of the remains ever made it into those boxes and coffins. They served as palatable props for a concerned public. Relatives who smelled a rat and became suspicious were warned of the possibility of hazardous bacteria and risks of exposure to contagions. Authorities tightened the screws another turn by not permitting the public anywhere near exhumation sites, only the transfer sites.

The rare handful of persistent relatives demanding to witness the entire exhumation and re-burial were confronted by aggressive teams of burly men in yellow hazmat suits. Their standard response, the one scripted by their supervisors, was mumbled from deep within the cloak of their biohazard headgear: 'Your loved ones are being handled with the utmost care and compassion. They can be visited at the transfer site.' Anyone visiting the transfer site would see a cheery new cemetery filled with fresh new graves, sealed, marked and sodded.

Rest in Peace.

As for Charlie Nickles? He protested and was told if he loved his new dream job and valued his benefits and pension, he'd keep his trap shut. Of course, Mayor Smythe, fresh from his latest three hour lunch break at The Golden Anchor, jumped into the fray with his eighty-proof input. "Don't think of this as a violation, Charlie, think of it as progress. And we all know you can't stop progress. It's inevitable."

Nickles hated Smythe for reducing sacred human lives to something so cheap and selfish. He spent a weekend in tortured reclusion debating his next move. *Should he report what he'd seen? Who should he report it to? And how?* He'd need some shit-solid proof. After three sleepless nights and a blinding, gin-fueled hangover, he did the math—sixty years old, four years to a full-pension retirement, a crumbling job market and nowhere else to go. He clammed up.

CHAPTER 25

The mayor loved to try and tweak Nickles by puking up the past and smearing it all over his face and neck. Mayor Smythe liked to think he had the upper hand, but Nickles knew he was just doling out his own personal form of paltry and perverse blackmail. During the arms race, cold war combatants called it 'assured mutual destruction' and the concept was simple: I kill you, you kill me, nobody wins. Nickles wasn't having any of it. He was happy to leave Smythe at The Golden Anchor, doing the backstroke through a pool of scotch and drowning in his own misery. Smythe could pickle his giblets and toss out all the empty threats he wanted, Nickles had work to do. Sheriff Riley and his deputies were big boys, they could fend for themselves, at least for awhile. Meanwhile, he had unfinished business with Kingfish.

It took Nickles an extra twenty minutes to navigate the road back to Kingfish's shack. An overnight downpour had turned the one-lane gravel and dirt into a sloppy soup. He dodged a set of washouts and eased his cruiser to a stop at Kingfish's lane. The gate was double-chained and locked. Nickles cut the engine, piled out and checked his pistol. It was loaded and ready.

He climbed the gate and made his way up the muddy, rutted lane to the shack. The swampy soil sucked at his boots, twice pulling them off his feet, socks and all. When he got to the shack, he found it locked up too. The stench from fish guts and cooked turtle meat was heavy in the air. Nickles heard noises at the back of the shack—muffled thumps and metallic scratches. He spotted a long, deep galvanized tank. It was partially covered with a camouflage net. There was a heavy steel lid on top with a boulder securing it in place.

Nickles pulled back the net and removed the boulder. The lid began to bounce. He pushed it back enough to reveal one dark corner of the tank. He drew closer. He could hear shrill hissing coming from deep within the opening. He leaned down. A pair of steely green eyes flashed in the darkness of the opening. There was a sound like bamboo smacking a dry pine board, then more hissing. A hungry mouth popped up, nipping a tiny piece of flesh from the side of Nickles' hand. Turtles. He picked up a stick, shoved the head away and scanned the darkened interior with his Maglite. The tank was full, alive with clawing, scratching, hissing snapping turtles. Nickles estimated fifty, maybe sixty in all. He closed the lid and replaced the boulder.

Next to the tub of turtles was a decaying clapboard shed. Mounted to the far end, under a moldy burlap canopy was a workbench constructed of rough-hewn planks and railroad ties. The benchtop was loaded with an enormous collection of vicious and brutal implements of intense pain and annihilation—Kingfish's kill bench. Nickles cast a nervous eye over the rusty tools—gaffing hooks, butcher knives, fish scalers, hatchets, a power drill with a corkscrew bit, sledgehammers, needle-nosed pliers, steel spikes, a blow torch, a vise, a fire axe and a chainsaw—a poachers playground. A light spray of fresh blood coated the splintered planks and corroded implements. Two dozen turtle heads, cleanly hacked from their bodies, lay in a drip pan under the jaws of the bloody bench vise.

Nickles checked the cabin. It was closed up tight. There was a sloppily written note tacked on the back door: **GOnE FiShIn'. YeR TREssPASSIn'. GiT OFF My PRopahTee!!!** Nickles fingered the note. He wondered what the hell Kingfish was up to and how long he'd been gone. His cell phone chirped. He punched it up. "Yeah."

"Where you at?"

The speech was slurred, the voice was panicked. Smythe.

"Why?"

"Got an update…'s important. 'Spose to be lookin' for Riley…"

Nickles waited.

"You shtill there."

"I'm here."

There was a crash on the other end of the phone, the sound of glass breaking and someone swearing. "Bunch of hunters 'spose to've seen Riley out on the lake…jus sittin' in the boat…"

Nickles let out a chuckle. "Probably lost."

"Why you have to make…dammit, get me a fresh drink…shtop being a wise ass Charlie…'

"Listen Mayor. Just shut up for a minute and listen to me."

Silence.

"I'm going back out on that lake and what I'll probably find is Sheriff Riley and two dipshit deputies trying to figure out where all the water is coming from. I find anything else, I'll let you know. Meantime, do me and Vivid Valley a huge favor."

"Whuzzat?"

"Sober the hell up!"

Nickles didn't wait for the Mayor's swollen-tongued reply. He clicked off, pocketed the cell phone and took another look at Kingfish's note. "Shit." Now he had a poacher and a Sheriff's Department to track down.

CHAPTER 26

Harld Money staggered through the woods, bouncing off rocks and trees as he made his way to the lake. He was out of breath and his ankle was weeping blood from a cut he received when he stumbled into a groundhog hole. He was beginning to hate making 'night runs' to Vivid Valley Lake, but it couldn't be helped. It was a necessary evil—a price he had to pay for cooking moonshine.

Money considered it shear genius. He cooked up the moonshine in his barn. The sour mash was filtered and tapped into gallon jugs. From there, Money carried it to the lake under cover of darkness. In the cove, he'd made a rock-lined pool near the shore. He could sink as many as thirty gallons just below the water's surface undetected. The hiding spot was ideal. It provided a cool place to store the liquor and it was off his property to keep the law off his ass. He didn't see the harm, it was just one more of Vivid Valley Lake's little secrets.

He made his way to a stump and flopped down. Sweat dripped from his eyebrows and stung his eyes. Over his panting he could hear ducks out on the lake—and loud splashing—probably a turtle lunging at a frog. He wanted a smoke, but didn't dare risk lighting a match and giving away his position. Instead, he fished out a wrinkled pack of chewing tobacco, unrolled it and packed an apple-sized wad in his jaw. The nicotine fix would hold him until he returned his jugs and was back at the barn. He pocketed the tobacco and pulled out his hip flask, a little nip to fight off the chilly night air.

When he'd drank his fill, he capped the flask and wobbled to his feet. The lake was reflecting the light of a full moon. He followed it like a landing beacon. His boots sucked at the waterlogged ground and his ankle throbbed. He cursed the groundhogs for burrowing holes into his hillsides to trip him up. The liquor fueled Money's anger and he began crashing through the underbrush, eager to get to the water and take care of business. At last he stumbled to the edge of a steep bank, nearly tumbling over the edge at breakneck speed. His hand snagged a sapling and he caught his balance. The drop down to the water was steeper than he remembered and for a moment he thought he was lost. He reached for his hip flask and took another shot of courage.

The lake was quiet now and the ducks had gone. He was alone. Slowly, he released the sapling. He slid down the muddy bank and waded out to his stash. The cool water soothed his bloody, twisted ankle. Knee-deep in the lake, he dipped his hands into the water, then pulled them back out. There was a strange current swirling around his hiding pool. The water churned, exposing a flash of black and green. He froze in his tracks. The water rippled and a flurry of bubbles appeared. Blood leaked from his injured ankle and mixed with the bubbles. A putrid stench surrounded Money. A lump broke the surface, then disappeared.

Money's eyes widened in shock. There was something down there. He stared into the water, trying to wrap his mind around the thing staring back at him. One eye pierced him to his soul; the other floated limp and dead in its socket. Money's eyes welled up as the thing swam closer. He thrust his hand into the water, found a boulder and chucked it. The thing didn't spook. It showed no fear. Money grabbed another rock and heaved it at the mutated head. This one connected.

Money's heart raced. He moved to the left, the thing swam left. He moved to the right, the thing swam right. He reached for his belt knife. His hand never got to the sheath. The creature leapt from the water and attacked. The yellow teeth latched on, sinking deep into Money's abdomen. Money stumbled backwards with the creature still firmly attached. Blood gushed from his severed flesh and mingled with the creature's undead hide.

As the thing continued to chomp, Money beat at its swollen head with his fists. His screams echoed through the cove. He swatted at the dead eye. The jaws tore through his neck. Money vomited a stream of blood through his quivering lips. The jaws took a final bite, severing Money's head. It toppled from his shoulders and rolled into the lake. The creature fed. The creature left.

CHAPTER 27

Nickles had been on the lake for over an hour. He'd cruised the entire southern and eastern section, trolling the inlets and coves and scanning the open water through binoculars. Nothing. The west had yielded nothing more than an abandoned canoe and a bass boat full of drunken, sunburned fisherman. He decided to make a pass around the northern inlets. If nothing turned up, he'd hang it up and call in some help from the State boys. The Staties had certified divers and sonic locators, all the fancy gizmos his department couldn't budget.

He was three miles off Grant's Cove when he spotted it—an aging, nuclear blue pontoon boat with a ragged canopy, a dented hull and twisted railings. A Party Barge. And there, tied up alongside, was Kingfish's boat. It was butted against the hull of the party boat, drifting sideways in the mouth of the cove. Nickles cruised in slow, coming up on the opposite side of the pontoon, hoping to stay on Kingfish's blind side. He caught a whiff of wild peppermint and something metallic and noxious as he tied off his boat and boarded the pontoon.

He found Kingfish standing over a twenty-something kid sprawled out on the deck of the pontoon. The kid's face was badly sunburned and his chest and legs were caked with dried blood and mangled bits of flesh. His blistered lips were quivering and his hands were trembling, still wrapped around the upper torso of a young woman.

Kingfish was visibly shaken. There were pellets of sweat breaking out on his forehead and his face was pale as two-percent milk. He pointed to the corpse, then turned to Nickles. "I found him just like that. He says she's his girlfriend, Liv." Kingfish stared down at the mess. "She ain't much of anything now."

"What the hell happened here?" asked Nickles.

"Beats me."

"You have anything to do with this?"

Kingfish balked. "Look, pal, I may be a whole lot of things, but I ain't no slasher and I *damned sure ain't a murderer*."

"So what gives, then?"

"I came up on this floating pile of junk and this is what I found. No more, no less."

Nickles watched the kid cradling the torso in his arms, gently rocking it back and forth. "He say anything?"

"So far, other than the bit about his girlfriend, the kid ain't said shit, just a lot of blubberin' and snortin'."

Nickles scanned the deck of the pontoon, littered with bottles and cans and a bag of something leafy and dull green that looked like pot. "Fucking party pinks."

The kid began babbling in loud, slobbery sobs, the shock setting in full tilt. Nickles stepped over the gore and knelt next to him. "What's your name, son?"

"A...Ar...Artie."

"Artie, what happened here?"

Artie's sun-blistered lips trembled. "Th...Thirsty."

Kingfish fetched a canteen from his boat and handed it to Nickles. Artie snatched it and struggled to uncap it and put it to his lips.

"Easy," said Nickles. "Take small sips."

Artie tipped the canteen and took a drink. Most of it came back up, soaking his shirt and shorts. He tried again. The water stayed down.

"Okay", said Nickles, "tell me what happened."

"It...It came out of the cove...killed them all...nev...never stood a chance."

"Slow down. What came out of the cove?"

Artie took another drink. He let out a belch and caught his breath. "A fish, well...at least I think it was a fish. We...I...I've never seen anything like it." He threw his hands apart in a wide gap. "Hu...huge mutant head, ugly gray and green body, rott...rotted fins, a left eye the color of buttermilk...an...and the smell, it was vile and sickening."

"You sure you saw a fish?" asked Kingfish.

Artie's head bobbed up and down. "It…its mouth was around Zig's head before he could get back to the boat. Those huge yellow teeth…God I'll never forget…it…they tore right through him."

"Yellow teeth?" Asked Nickles.

Artie took another gulp of water and padded his swollen lips with the back of his hand. "All I kept thinking was: 'This thing shouldn't be alive.' And, you know…it…I don't think it was alive. I think it…"

Nickles waited.

Artie choked.

"Go ahead, Artie, what do you think?"

"I…I think it was a monster."

Nickles felt the yellow tooth stashed in his pocket, let his hand drift to its jagged edge for a moment. "You're telling me you think it was dead? That you were attacked by a dead fish?"

Artie shook his head, sending sweat and slobber off his face in a wide arch. "Not dead, undead."

Nickles bit his lip. "I see. And this undead thing, it attacked— what was his name again?"

"Zig. It killed him. I…It…just mangled him…ate him alive. It got Juice and Liv too."

Kingfish leaned in close to Nickles' ear. "You ain't buyin' this dumb kid's monster fish story, are ya?"

Nickles looked out over the lake, then back at the bloody remains scattered around the deck of the pontoon. "I'm not sure what I believe. One thing's for sure, we got a dead girl here and somebody killed her."

"No…not *somebody*." Artie interrupted. *"Something*. Don't you get it? We were attacked!" He pointed in the direction of Grant's Cove. "And that thing…that monster…it's still out there…somewhere."

Kingfish shook his head. "Could be dope. Damn lake is full of partiers. Who knows what all they been eatin', snortin', shootin' and drinkin'? I've seen little shits like this one get all jacked up and go looney tunes before. Bet you have too."

Nickles leaned over the edge of the boat and checked the mangled ladder still dangling in the water. "Yep, I've seen a little bit of just about everything since this lake came along." He looked back at Artie, still clutching the top half of Liv's corpse, then back down at the ladder. "If this kid's high, that's one thing. Still don't explain this though."

Kingfish looked where Nickles was pointing. There was a wide, circular chunk missing from the top step of the ladder and eight deep puncture marks in the aluminum pontoon. "Shit."

"Ever seen anything like that before?" asked Nickles.

Kingfish reached down and slid three fingers in one of the punctures holes. There was room to spare. He flashed back to the ugly creature that ate Billy Mize while his brain constructed a believable lie. "Ain't from no turtle, that's for damned sure." He eyed the piece missing from the ladder. "And I don't even wanna think about a fish big enough to take a bite that big. The teeth would be enormous."

"And vicious," said Nickles. He pulled the yellow tooth from his pocket and thrust it into one of the punctures. It was a perfect fit. He held it up to Kingfish. "Something like this."

Kingfish stared at the tooth, then plucked it from Nickles' fingers. It was bigger than the ones that tore through Billy's throat. "Yer dreamin', pal. Ain't nothin' like that swimmin' in Vivid Valley Lake."

Arite caught a glimpse of the tooth and began to freak. His face turned ash white as his eyes welled up. "Th...tha...that's what got Zig. G...got Juice and Liv too. It wa... it was a monster." He pointed to the tooth in Kingfish's hand. "A monster wi...with a mouthful of those."

Nickles snatched the tooth away from Kingfish and shoved the razor edge under his nose. "You telling me you've never seen teeth like this?"

There was a trickle of blood seeping from the tip of Kingfish's nose."That's what I'm tellin' ya."

Nickles' face hardened. His bullshit detector was going off. "Kingfish, you need to think real hard before you answer my next question. Back at your shack you got enough fish and game violations to land your ass in lock-up for a nice long stretch."

"Look, Nickles, I don't like where this is headed. I come out here on the lake, I find this kid sprawled out on the deck of a shitbeater party barge with the top half of his date cradled in his arms and kibbles-n-bits spattered all over hell and you wanna roust me? You wanna charge me with somethin', then get to it. I got shit to do and babysittin' some wet-behind-the-ears doper who wigged out and hacked up his party pals ain't one of 'em. I stopped to help. It ain't appreciated, I'm gone."

Nickles wiggled the tooth, nudging it into the tip of Kingfish's nose again. "You're not leaving, not till I get some answers."

Kingfish pulled back from the tooth.

"In your shack," continued Nickles, "up on a high shelf, I saw a jarful of these yellow teeth—smaller, but they were the same damn teeth."

"So? Ain't no law against keepin' teeth in a damned jar, least none I know of."

"Yeah, I forgot, you *know* the fish and game laws. You just never cared enough to follow them."

Kingfish stared at the bloody mess on the deck of the pontoon. Artie had released Liv, gotten to his feet, stumbled to the rail and was barfing into the water. His legs were shaking as his back arched from the heaving.

"The teeth," said Nickles, "they're the same as this one—same shape, same color, same sharp edge—and they came from something. You know what it is." He gave the tooth another nudge, pushing it close enough to break the skin. "Now, take a good, long look, stow the bullshit and tell me what the hell I'm dealin' with."

"I'm tellin' you, nothin' on this lake is sproutin' choppers that big. No way."

"And I'm telling you there is. Now spill it."

Kingfish rubbed a filthy palm across his forehead. "That can't be. Those teeth in my jar? They came from Gar. Ain't no Gar I've seen that would grow that big. It ain't possible. No way."

Nickles pointed the tip of the tooth towards the lake. "Yes way—the teeth marks on this boat, the bloody mess covering the deck, a petrified party boy cuddling with pieces of his butchered dead girlfriend, convinced an undead monster has eaten his pals— it's possible." Nickles watched Artie heave another load into the water. "Look at him, he's scared shitless and convinced a huge monster fish is behind it."

"Not a Gar. They don't grow that big naturally."

"How do you explain this, then?" asked Nickles, eyeing the yellow tooth."

"If that's from a Gar, then something out in that lake is makin' 'em that big—something unnatural. Explain that away."

Now it was Nickles' turn to lie. "There's nothing in that lake but water."

"And some godawful thing with a mouthful of those," said Kingfish, pointing at the tooth.

Nickles shoved the tooth back in his pocket. The same instant, Artie let out a high-pitched yelp and the pontoon began to rock violently. Nickles turned in time to see the creature leap from the water and latch onto Artie's torso. The force knocked him off his feet. He scrambled backwards, slicing his arm on a broken tequila bottle as the creature arched high in the air and vanished below the surface, taking Artie's upper half with him.

"You believe it now?" asked Nickles.

Before Kingfish could answer, the thing was back, attacking the pontoons with rabid chomps. The boat began to list, as the punctured pontoons flooded with lake water. Nickles drew his ,45 and emptied the clip into the creatures slimy, bulbous head. It continued to chomp. The boat continued to sink. Nickles reloaded and continued to fire.

Kingfish had tied off on one side of the pontoon, Nickles on the other. They each struggled to get to their lines, desperate to keep their boats from being pulled under by the sinking party pontoon. Nickles' injured arm spurted blood, coating the deck of the pontoon with more gore. He dashed back to his boat. The lines were becoming tangled. He worked at the twisted bundle of knots, yanking hard to keep as much of the line above water as possible. It was no use, the pontoon was swiftly slipping below the surface, dragging Nickles and his boat down with it. He shouted at Knigfish, who was busy fighting with his own lines. He had a folding knife in his hand and was dangling over the edge of his boat, inches from the churning water.

He reached down, flicked the knife open and cut his lines. He was loose. He fired the motor and hit the throttle. The wake threw a plume of water over the sinking pontoon, taking it down another foot. Kingfish circled Nickles' boat as it began to capsize. Nickles loaded a fresh clip in the .45 and shifted the muzzle between the creature's head and Kingfish's head. Kingfish punched the throttle and circled again. Nickles took aim. His finger tightened on the trigger waiting for Kingfish to come back around and fill his sights.

"Come on man," shouted Kingfish over the roar of his boat motor. "It's a loss." He throttled back and let the boat glide in close. "You got no choice. Jump!"

Nickles switched targets and put three more slugs in the creature's head. He holstered the .45, braced himself against the rail of his boat and leapt onto Kingfish's boat. Kingfish hit the throttle as Nickles' boat and the pontoon slipped below the surface.

CHAPTER 28

The creature darted in and out of the wreckage, snapping at bits and pieces of Artie's riddled body. It closed in on every morsel and still it craved more. It whipped the water into a bloody froth with its rotting fins and tail. And then it caught it—just below the surface, but not far away—a strong scent of fresh human prey.

The scent drifted into its undead gills and filled its scent glands. It swam toward the scent. The flesh smelled tender and full of life. Soon there were flashes of movement in the water above. Something young. Something tasty. A beach. It swam closer and opened its cavernous maw, exposing wicked yellow teeth.

The first one died quickly. The monster took him in deep water, floating on an inflatable that looked like a cartoon alligator. The creature bit through the cheap green vinyl and pierced the man's heart. There were no screams, no yelps of pain, just a rush of air escaping from the raft and a few splashes as the raft deflated and a bloody swimmer slipped beneath the surface.

The water around the beach was alive with prey—divers, swimmers, boaters, surfers on boogey boards, young, old, male, female—it was a frolicking feast of fresh flesh. The creature took it all in as it fed on the muscled thighs of swimmers. Then, it attacked with a vengeance. It took a blonde dog-paddling in the shallows. Her legs were torn away cleanly and she toppled over in the water like a fishing bobber. Horror filled her eyes as she swatted at the water and tried to right herself. Her fingers connected with the creature's milky dead eye as the yellow teeth connected with her neck.

Next, the creature scuttled a canoe, tossing the two teens into the lake. They broke the surface and began to swim. The youngest, a wiry scrap of shaggy hair and gangly limbs was off like a shot.

The other canoeist struggled, fighting against the ensuing panic. As he swam, his lungs began to burn and his heart pounded in his chest. He ducked below the surface and power-stroked toward the shore. Fifteen feet, maybe twenty and he'd be safe on dry land. He kicked his feet. The teeth connected with his skin. He yelled. His shouts were smothered by water filling his mouth and lungs.

Eventually the screaming started. As more and more blood floated to the surface and drifted ashore, panic began to set in. Swimmers scrambled out of the water and ran along the beach looking for someone, anyone to make it stop. A lifeguard dashed into the lake and was immediately consumed. A surfer on a boogey board leapt off and began smacking at the creature with the hard edge of the board. He got in two good licks to the creatures ruddy green back. Then the fight was over.

The creature ate its fill. The killing was easy. Death had become its sole purpose and it dealt it out willingly. As the beach was filled with bloody victims and useless shouting, the creature turned its rotting tail toward the shore and disappeared into the blackness below. When the hunger returned, it would too.

CHAPTER 29

They watched from a distance as both boats disappeared below the surface. Kingfish looked at Nickles' arm. "You okay?"

Nickles grunted. "I'll live. Figured you were going to leave me back there."

"Thought about it, I really did."

"Why didn't you?"

Kingfish shrugged. "Good question."

Nickles eyed the bleeding gash on his arm. "If it would've been me, I would've left you."

"Um hum."

"In a heartbeat."

There was a sinister grin blooming on Kingfish's face. "Appreciate your honesty."

"No problem."

Kingfish eyed the .45 still in Nickles hand. "Were you really gonna shoot me?"

"If I had to, I would have."

Kingfish watched the churning water where the boats sank. "Looks like we're in this together."

"Can't say I'm all that thrilled about it."

"Ditto. Could be worse, though. You could be feedin' that rotted, yellow toothed bastard right now." Kingfish pointed to a large metal lockbox bolted to the deck. "Got a first aid kit in there. You might wanna tend to that arm."

The flow of blood from Nickles' arm had slowed, but was still weeping from the gash and dripping off his fingertips. "It'll be okay."

"Suit yourself, but you don't know what kind of creepin crud that thing is carryin' around between its yellow teeth and rubbery lips. I'd lay odds on it bein' toxic. Might be even be something airborne. I was you, I wouldn't take a chance on the kind of infection that butt-ugly mother could dole out."

Nickles shook the droplets of blood off his fingers. "You ain't me."

"True enough."

Nickles checked his .45 and shoved in a fresh clip. "You get a good look at that ugly-faced sonofabitch? I must have put fifteen or twenty slugs in that thing. It didn't so much as belch."

"I think the kid was right, that thing is some sorta freak—a travesty of nature."

"It's not normal, that much is for sure." Nickles scanned the water, keeping an eye out for the mutated, bulbous head or a glimpse of the milky, dead eye. "That doesn't explain how it got that way."

Kingfish was quiet for a bit, letting his anger simmer while he put some distance between them and the sunken boats. He suddenly wanted to explode, tell Nickles everything, but wasn't sure he could trust him. After all that had happened, he wasn't sure they'd be alive much longer anyway. He remembered the ancient grounds he'd been forced to keep secret for all these years, the image of Billy being torn to shreds, Artie's frightened eyes as he'd clutched the remains of his mangled girlfriend, and the vicious creature responsible for it all. Finally, his cork popped. He turned and faced Nickles. "Damned crazy fools. I tried to tell 'em years ago, when this whole damned lake was just a glimmer in the bureaucrat's greedy eyes."

Nickles gave him a puzzled look. He figured Kingfish was headed for a crack-up. "What the hell are you talking about?"

Kingfish began to pace as he ranted. "Silly fools, they came traipsin' into this valley, stompin' over every square inch of it. Most of 'em were small men with big titles. They set up their surveyin' equipment, drove their wooden stakes, hung their little red ribbons, and for what? All in the name of progress."

Nickles watched Kingfish pace the deck and wave his arms frantically. "You going somewhere with this, or are you just letting off steam?"

Kingfish's face was flushed with anger. His jaw bunched and he spat into the lake. "Sonsofbitches took me for some backwater hillbilly. They didn't wanna hear about the graves, They didn't care."

Nickles' ears pricked. *Graves? Did he say graves? How could he know?*

"They thought I was just a turtle-eatin', country hick." Kingfish slapped himself on the chest. "Well, even this hick knows you don't mess with ancient burial grounds."

"Wait. What? What ancient burial grounds?"

Kingfish threw his hands in the air. "See, you don't know either, do ya?"

Nickles shook his head. "Suppose you humor me."

Kingfish had a disgusted look on his face. "Seriously? You never of the Moundbuilders?"

Nickles was relieved, but curious. If Kingfish didn't know about the abandoned cemetery plots, his secret was safe. Kingfish didn't say cemeteries. He'd used words like ancient and sacred. If he was right, and there were other bodies hidden under the lake, Nickles had a whole new secret to keep him up at night. He wasn't sure he wanted to hear it. He asked anyway. "Tell me."

Kingfish kept an eye on the horizon as he laid out his tale. "Adena. They were around before Christ himself, least ways the first ones were. They were moundbuilders. At one time there were mounds all around Vivid Valley. Some were ceremonial, most were burial grounds—what the archeologists called funerary earthworks. I knew where most of 'em were, even offered to point 'em out to those pinheads. They told me to mind my own business."

"How do you know all this?"

Kingfish spat in the lake again, watched the spit glob float away on the current. "Like I said, I ain't some dumb hick who parks his teeth in a water glass next to his bed at night. I can read. I see things. I hear things. I *know* things. Besides, my kin was in this valley before the civil war. They saw things too, and learned things, and respected things. Eventually, I raised such a stink the county decided to investigate. They sent some college professor from up-state. He had a bunch of his rock-pickin' students along for the ride."

Nickles had Kingfish's first aid kit out and was dousing the gash in his arm with peroxide, gritting his teeth as the bloody flesh bubbled. "What'd they do?" he grunted.

"They had me take them to the mounds. They musta' walked those earthworks for a solid week, measurin', explorin', takin' pictures and scratchin' their asses. Then, they mapped every square inch of 'em. The professor was all fired up about protectin' sacred soil and preservin' history. He said he aimed to escalate it all the way to Washington."

Washington. Nickles had a belly-full of government, enough to last a lifetime. He knew where Kingfish's secret story was going to end. At the bottom of Vivid Valley Lake, right next to his own, smothered by millions of gallons of water. "Shit."

"Double shit. And just like that," Kingfish snapped his calloused fingers, "they packed up their tape measures and notebooks and cameras and all their fancy gear and disappeared like ghosts."

"They never came back?"

"Never."

Nickles pursed his lips, let out a long, slow puff of air. "And that was the end of it?"

"Not quite. There's still the Mayor. I went to him before all the dozers and heavy earthmovers started rippin' this valley apart. I begged him to listen. He farted me off, sat down his tumbler of booze long enough to tell me how important this lake was, that it was progress and you can't fight progress." Kingfish sat again and wiped his chin. "All the good Mayor cared about was money. And if it meant takin' a shit on a huge chunk of history and defiling the ancient dead, it was no skin of his lily white ass."

Nickles gave his arm another splash of peroxide. "Fuckin' Smythe," he mumbled.

"Whatsat again?"

"Huh? Oh, nothing."

"Well, anyway, they went right ahead on and violated those ancient burial mounds. Now it's everybody's business."

"How so?"

"They dug into those mounds, disturbed the contents and stole sacred ritual artifacts. When they finished their looting and got bored with the mess they'd created, they walked away and let the lake have it. They had no idea the curse their meddling had created."

"Curse?"

Kingfish scanned the lake for signs of the mutant Gar. The water was calm. "It's Adena law. You desecrate their burial sites, an unholy curse is unleashed—a curse with a deadly outcome."

"How come I've never heard of these mounds? Or seen any of them?"

"You don't know what you're lookin' for, you'll never spot 'em. To an untrained eye they just look like a big 'ol heap of dirt or a hill. Far as the knowin' goes, you were still up in Pokagon earnin' your wings and roustin' hunters and fishermen. That was before the state transferred you down here to Vivid Valley and gifted you with your dream job."

Pokagon. How the hell did Kingfish know about that? And what else did he know?

Kingfish winked. "Told you I weren' t no dumb hilljack."

Nickles was still absorbing it all—the mutilated deer, the cemetery plots, the missing J & K tour boat, Mayor Smythe, Riley and his deputies, the man-eating creature and now, violated ancient burial grounds.

Kingfish gave him a nudge. "Get the distinct feelin' you ain't listenin'."

Nickles was listening, but his eyes were on the lake. That thing, that mutated Gar was still out there, somewhere. If it was strong enough to punch through a pontoon hull and take .45 rounds at close range, they were sitting ducks. "You tellin' me that thing out there is the result of some ancient curse?"

"Ain't sayin' it is, ain't sayin' it ain't." Kingfish turned and looked Nickles dead in the eyes. "Bet'choo got a few skeletons buried too, huh?"

"Why you say that?"

"Everybody does."

Nickles was quiet.

"Anyway, I do got me a bit of a confession to make."

Nickles gave the slice in his arm a final blast of peroxide and watched it bubble frothy, white foam. "I look like a priest to you?"

Kingfish barked out a laugh. "Nope, I 'spose you don't." He rubbed the stubble on his chin with his thumb and forefinger. "You asked me before if I got a good look at that thing."

"Yeah."

"Well, I've seen it before."

"You what? Where?"

"Couple days ago. Me and Billy, we were out runnin' turtle lines. That freakish beast that ate the kid, Artie? Well he done the same for Billy, just used those yellow teeth to shred him up into bite-size bits. It's bigger now. I don't know why, but I think it's growin', and fast."

"You're sure about this?"

"Same hideous yellow teeth, same half dead, rotting body, same putrid stench—it's the same critter alright. And I aim to hunt it down and destroy it."

"You said it ate Billy. We talking Billy Mize."

"None other."

"Mize," Nickles mumbled. Another Vivid Valley thorn in his side. Mize had sand for brains and a near lethal meth habit. He had a long history with cops. None of it was good. "Billy Jefferson Cromwell Mize. Good riddance to a bag of rubbish."

"He might've been rubbish to you," said Kingfish, "but he didn't deserve to go out like he did. And I aim to make it right. I'm not quitin' till I find that thing and send it swimming back to hell."

Nickles bristled. "Now hold up here. I got enough to deal with on this lake right now. The last thing I need is a renegade out on open water creating panic and killing anything that swims."

"Don't you get it? The first time I saw that rotted lump of meat was around Grant's Cove. Adena occupied that whole area ages ago. It was their land before it was anyone's. We violated sacred soil. Their sacred soil. That thing out there is the end result. It's not a fish any more, not a Gar. It's a mutated, undead monster and it's carryin' around a gut full of human meat and an ancient curse."

"You honestly believe that?"

"You *don't?*"

Before Nickles could answer, his cell phone chirped. Mayor Smythe. "What now?"

"There's been some kind of an attack at Crescent Beach. We got at least two dead, maybe more. Get there fast."

Nickles didn't reply, just clicked off and flipped the cell shut. "This shit just keeps getting better."

"What?"

"I'm going to need your boat. I'll drop you at the shoreline and see to it you get home."

Kingfish threw a hand into Nickles' chest. "Hold up, there hoss. Where my boat goes, I go, and ain't no lousy fish cop gonna take over my boat and leave me hoofin' it home. Not now, not ever."

Nickles unzipped his jacket and pointed to his shield with the barrel of his .45.

"Badge flipper."

CHAPTER 30

Nickles took the controls and fired the engine on Kingfish's boat. He slapped the throttle, causing the twin props to scoop up lake water in deep, foaming troughs.

"You bung up my boat, the DNR'll be gettin' a hefty bill."

Nickles winked. "Relax, I'm a professional."

"Um hum."

"Where you want me to drop you?"

Kingfish rubbed his bristled chin with the back of his hand. "Been thinkin' a great deal on that. I'd kinda like to know your intentions."

"Intentions? I'm going to the beach, sort this whole mess out and kill that yellow-toothed monster. Then, me and Mayor Smythe, we're going to have a long, serious chat about his future."

"About time somebody took on that knucklehead." Kingfish let a burst of spray from the lake drench his face and chest. He relished the cool water as it dripped from his chin and soaked through his shirt. "This thing is gonna be a handful. Might be best if you called in some serious reinforcements."

Nickles stayed on the throttle, aiming the boat towards shore. "Won't be any reinforcements."

"Whysat?"

Nickles was silent.

They crossed a heavy wake, launching the boat high in the air and slapping it back into the water. A wave sliced across the deck and rocked the hull. The engine sputtered, then caught again.

Kingfish pressed. "Nickles, why ain't there no reinforcements?"

Nickles' face hardened. "Sheriff Riley? His deputies? They're all MIA. I was out here looking for them when I found you and the kid."

They were both quiet, each thinking the same thing about Riley and his crew, knowing it was probably true. Nickles got to the shoreline and eased back on the throttle. The boat buffered against a low bank of tree roots and mud. "This will have to do. I get things squared, I'll be back for you. Hop off."

The smirk reappeared on Kingfish's face. "You goin' after that undead thing with just a handgun and a pocket full of bullets? You really do have a death wish, don'tcha?"

"Maybe. Maybe not. What's it to you? You'll be out of the line of fire."

"You seen the same thing I did. Poppin' that monster with a .45 was like smackin' it with a fly swatter."

Nickles stared at the .45, half empty and only one spare magazine for back-up. Everything else was on his boat at the bottom of Vivid Valley Lake.

Kingfish leaned in close, put a hand on Nickles' shoulder. "If I was goin' after that thing, I mean really goin' for the kill, I'd be armed to the teeth and ready for the apocalypse."

Nickles let the boat idle as he stared out over the lake—the lake that was now home to abandoned graves, ancient funerary mounds, his boat, a mutant killer creature and everything he needed to hunt and kill it. There was a hollow feeling deep in his stomach. His gut rumbled. The caustic juices stirred, eating away at his backbone.

Kingfish squeezed Nickles' shoulder. It was a light touch, just enough to get his attention. "Anybody chasin' that thing down better be packin' heavy. That is, unless they got a powerful desire to see the inside of that undead piece of shit up close and personal."

Nickles patted the butt of his .45. "I got no choice, I gotta go with what I got."

There was a sudden twinkle of mischief in Kingfish's eyes. "Gotcha covered, hoss." He flipped open a metal hatch on the deck of the boat. "Behold."

Nickles peered through the hatch at the arsenal of weapons as Kingfish rattled off his inventory. "We got a Remington Express with one case each of deer slugs and double aught buckshot, twin Desert Eagles in .44 mag with a thousand rounds to keep 'em fed and happy." He hefted a fifteen inch machete. "And of course, we got a few edged weapons just in case things get intimate."

Nickles looked closer. "Is that a Barrett .50 caliber?"

"It is."

"You got a permit for it?"

Kingfish threw his hands up. His eyes played over Nickles a second, then looked away. "It never stops with you, does it?"

Nickles didn't answer, just took inventory of Kingfish's cache. His eyes locked on a triangular, black case. What's in there?"

Kingfish's chest swelled. "A little somethin' special."

"Like what?"

Kingfish popped the latches on the case and opened the lid. "Ain't she a beauty?"

"What the hell is it?"

Kingfish hoisted the contraption out of the case. To Nickles, it looked like a cobbled together pile of washing machine parts, brake drums, bicycle wheels, steel cable and twisted bits of scrap metal. "Where in God's name did you get that?"

Kingfish cracked a wicked smile and elbowed Nickles. He hoisted the weapon to his shoulder. "Built her myself. I call her Ardetta." He notched a steel rod in the receiver, twisted a metal knob to set the tension and fired it at an old growth walnut tree thirty feet inland. The rod punched through the trunk, splitting it in half before plowing into a distant hillside. The force kicked up a shower of dirt and rocks that rained down on the lake in thick clumps. "Any questions?"

"Just one."

Kingfish cocked an eyebrow.

"Why'd you name it Ardetta?"

Kingfish let out a snort. "'Cause that 'ol gal was the meanest bitch ever to haunt this here valley."

"She do you wrong?"

"Shit. Ardetta, she done *everybody* wrong."

Nickles eyed the damage done by Ardetta. The walnut tree was disintegrated. Not a splinter remained in place. "Ardetta," he mumbled.

Kingfish rubbed a palm over Ardetta's smooth steel frame. "She's all yours. Just one catch."

"No."

"Come on. Much as you hate to admit it, you need me. That thing out there gets hungry and breaks the surface again, it'll hit hard and fast. You need someone to ride shotgun." Kingfish put Ardetta back in her case, picked up the 870 Express and racked the action. "Face it, I'm your man."

"No."

"I told ya this once before. It bears repeatin'. You and me, we're stuck with each other. That butt ugly fish-thing saw to that. The way I see it, we can either die tryin' to kill that thing by ourselves, or help each other out. Either way, we's in this thing together."

Nickles' stomach rumbled again. He'd spent the last six years trying to comb Kingfish out of his hair and get him to follow the law. Now he had to depend on him and a cache of illegal weapons to protect him, maybe even save his life.

Kingfish gave him another elbow to the ribs. "What's it gonna be, hoss? We gonna fish or we gonna cut bait?"

Nickles took his hand off the butt of the .45 and took another look at Kingfish and the cache of weapons. Without them, he was doomed. With them, he might just have a fighting chance. He throttled up and turned the boat away from shore. "Hang on."

CHAPTER 31

Nickles slammed the throttle to full, launching Kingfish on his ass. The boat knifed through the water, sending a fine spray rooster-tailing behind them in a high, wide arch. While Nickles kept the boat on course, Kingfish readied his weapons and searched the lake for any signs of the mutant. They were two miles from the beach when he spotted it—something bulbous and round bobbing in the water. He raised his binoculars and motioned for Nickles to slow down.

"Is it the creature?"

Kingfish fiddled with the focus on his binoculars. "Don't think so. Whatever it is, it ain't movin', just floatin'."

"Maybe it's playing dead."

"Or undead."

Nickles drew his .45. "We're going in slow. It makes a move, we nail it. You ready?"

Kingfish lowered his binoculars and racked a deer slug into the shotgun. "Shazam."

Nickles trolled the boat in slowly, circling the thing from eighty feet, then sixty, then forty. There was no sign of movement, just a floating blob riding the waves. He inched back the throttle and let the boat coast in—twenty feet, fifteen feet, ten, five. "Holy shit!"

Kingfish lowered the shotgun and poked the lump with the barrel. It bobbed up and down, then rolled over in the choppy water. Kingfish let out a low groan as Hearld Money's face appeared. His head and neck had been mangled like a chew toy. "Where the hell's the rest of him?" asked Kingfish.

"Beats me."

"You reckon that thing ate Hearld?"

Nickles let out a nervous laugh. "If it did, it'll be stone drunk for a solid month."

Kingfish gave Money's severed head another poke. "Yep, appears as if 'Ol Hearld has cooked his last batch of Vivid Valley moon." He watched Hearld Money's head bob-n-weave in the gentle current. "Poor, sorry bastard. That thing done turned him into a human beach ball."

"What's worse," said Nickles, "That old drunk probably never knew what hit him."

Kingfish stared at the terror-filled eyes in Money's severed head. "Or maybe he did." He gave the head one last poke, watching it disappear below the surface. "What now?"

"Nothing we can do for Hearld Money that hasn't already been done. Let's get to the beach."

The beach. After the carnage he'd seen the last few days, Kingfish didn't want to think about it. He just wanted it to stop.

CHAPTER 32

The scene laid out on the beach was like a bloody battlefield. Pieces of bodies, ripped-up legs and arms and torn bits of flesh were scattered on the sandy shore and floating along on the bloody tide. The monster had eaten away most of the flesh, leaving the rest to bloat and rot. Nickles and Kingfish drifted through the carnage, searching for any survivors. There were none.

An unholy stench bubbled up from the bottom of the lake—the smell of disease, sulfur, decay and death—ancient death. The sickening odor wafted over the beach in a thick green cloud, making Nickles wretch. "Damn."

Kingfish did a palm-wave in front of his face like he was shooing off a pesky, green fly. "It's a might potent, ain't it?"

Nickles heaved into the shallow water and wiped his chin. "Potent isn't the word for it."

Kingfish chuckled.

"You been around some pretty vile stuff in your life," said Nickles, watching the noxious green cloud drift along the beach. "You ever, in all your days of poaching and piddling, smelled anything that horrible?"

"Live or dead?"

"Does it matter?"

"'Spose not." Kingfish propped a foot on the deck rail and spat into the lake. He stared at the smelly green cloud and let his eyes narrow. "When I was just a snot-nosed little shit, we lived in a big 'ol house up near Goose Knob. My Pop rented the back half of that house to an old man name of Pesky Wexler."

"Goofy name," Nickles grunted.

"Yeah, it is, ain't it? Anyway, Pesky, he was a real loner—kept to hisself, fended for hisself, even talked to hisself. After a while, he started to hate hisself. That's when he decided to check out."

"Check out? You saying what I think you're saying?"

Kingfish cleared his throat and spit into the lake again, trying to get the foul taste out of his mouth. "Yep, the big out. He hung hisself in his closet. It was in the middle of August, no air conditioning or fans. Hell, we could barely afford electricity. It bein' that swelterin' hot, Pesky got exceedingly ripe by the time we found him. Rigor had set in and he had the dead juice dripping from the toes of his filthy socks. Maggots were workin' him over real good too."

Nickles wretched again. "Why you telling me this?"

"Gettin' to that, just need a minute." Kingfish took a red handkerchief from his pocket, blew his nose and turned to face Nickles. "Pesky, he never was much for hygiene, so he had a head start on workin' up a pretty good stink long before he offed himself. Nature and the Good Lord took care of the rest. I carried that odor around for years, just couldn't get it out of my nose or my brain." He pointed at the growing green cloud. "Now I got me a whole new stench to fuck me up and it makes that old man's swingin' corpse smell like a big city flower and garden show.

Nickles thought about the source of that stench, the real reasons for the carnage littering Vivid Valley Lake. And all of it could have been prevented. He could have prevented it. There was a cold, hard lump lodged deep in his belly and it scraped at his intestines like a wad of steel wool. "Tell me everything you know about the Adena."

"Ya mean besides what I already told ya?"

"Everything."

Kingfish stared at the mess floating past them in the bloody water. "They was on this good earth from around 1000 B.C. to 100 A.D., so they didn't leave no written records—not like we do. Their history was left on the land, writ in dirt and stone. Adena were people of honor. Along with the dearly departed, the graves in those mounds were filled with treasures."

"I thought you said—."

"That they had no value," Kingfish interrupted. "And they didn't, least not to me and you."

"What were they, then?"

"Beads, amulets, copper bracelets, arrow heads, clay pipes—all the prized possessions of the deceased. Religious beliefs of a burial cult demanded it as part of the ritual."

Nickles' face twisted. "Cult?"

"Not a cult like you and I think of it. Weren't none of that Jim Jones tripe, nor Hale Bop Comet bullshit. The Adena were a cult of the honored dead."

"Which means?"

"Which means they though as much of their people when they'd passed as they did when they were alive. Was a time when we use to do that too. Well, when we cut into those mounds and looted them, we dishonored the Adena."

Nickles steered the boat away from a mangled swimmer. "You keep saying we, like we're the ones who caused all this."

Kingfish held up a hand. "Now, don't go takin' that personal. Hell, we might not have started this bizarre barn dance ourselves, but modern man sure did. Those burial crypts underneath this lake was ruined by packs of clod bustin' treasure hunters. They didn't think of it as a violation. They tacked a big 'ol fancy term on it to help hide their shame. They called it archeological salvage. Ain't that a kick in the head?"

Nickles shook his head in disgust.

"Them treasure hunters tore into those mounds a shovel-load at a time, collectin' up scraps of bone, skull, artifacts, anything they could dust off and toss in a sack. They ravaged those mounds like a sewer rat rootin' through a city dumpster. Once they realized there weren't nothin' in 'em they could profit from, they set out to find more so they could tear 'em up just for fun. Eventually, society just ignored the mounds all together—buildin' roads over 'em, plowing them under with farm tractors," Kingfish thrust his hands in front of him as another severed leg drifted by, "or in this case, flooded 'em under millions of gallons of water."

Nickles half expected Kingfish to bust out a laugh, to tell him it was just a country boy joke to get under his skin and make him look foolish. There was no buck-snorting chuckle, no rooster cackle, no shit eating grin of deception. Kingfish's face was stone. "That's it, then? That's the cause of this man eating abomination in Vivid Valley Lake"

"Appears as if."

"You got any more good news?"

Kingfish tilted his neck from side-to-side, feeling the joints crack. "This next part is folklore, more of a legend, actually. Adena held tight to the beliefs of the sacred powers of nature. They was a clannish bunch, too. And them clans each lived under the sign of a tribal beast. The beasts were usually chosen by the tribal chiefs. They were idols, a sign of a tribe's character and strength."

"What kind of beasts?"

"It varied—eagles, deer, owls, frogs, snakes—."

"And?"

"Fish and turtle. If you believe the legends, it appears the clans in these parts was right partial to fish and turtles. They used 'em in blood rituals to invoke the spirits."

"Great."

A life preserver bobbed in the water near the bow of the boat. Kingfish reached down to pull it in before he realized there was someone in it. She was eight, maybe nine years old, wearing a once piece bathing suit and very dead. "Son, we gotta stop this thing, 'fore it kills every living thing in Vivid Valley."

Nickles watched the life preserver drift out of view. "Agreed." He nodded toward the bodies strewn along the beach. "You got any ideas on how to go about it so we don't end up like them?"

Kingfish slapped his knee. "Thought you'd never ask. Try this one on for size. You wanna catch a fish, right? Whattaya do?"

Nickles wrinkled his brow. "Kingfish, we don't have time for twenty questions here."

"Serious, whattaya do?"

"I give up."

Kingfish retrieved a grappling hook from the deck and fished a floating torso out of the water. He hauled it on deck and flopped it over. "Ya gotta bait 'em."

"You can't be serious."

"I am." Kingfish pointed to the gash in Nickles' arm. "Gonna need some of your blood, though." He drew his knife from the sheath and split the torso open. "Put a little right in there."

Nickles balked. "After all this talk about dishonoring the dead? No damned way."

"Suit yourself. I don't like it any more than you do. You got a better idea, I'm all ears."

Nickles eyed the split torso and chewed his cheek.

"Well?"

"Give me a minute, I'm thinking."

"Um hum, I thought I smelled smoke."

"Up yours." Nickles stared at the mangled corpse, wondering how he'd let things get this out-of-hand. He swore if he lived through it, he'd thrash Mayor Curtis Smythe within an inch of his drunken life. Then, he'd put some serious distance between himself and Vivid Valley. "Okay, what do we do?"

"First, yer blood, then we cast the dearly departed out behind the boat and start tollin' the open waters."

"Then what?"

"Damned if I know. I'm makin' this up as we go."

Nickles held his arm over the torso and squeezed out some blood. "Marvelous."

Soon, Kingfish had the torso trussed up on the grappling hook and attached to a length of steel cable. He fed it out in a straight line behind the boat and secured it to a turnbuckle. He told Nickles to keep the boat moving in a slow, straight path across the lake.

"Now what?"

Kingfish let the cable reel out all the way. "Now, we watch and we wait."

CHAPTER 33

The creature was just below the surface, watching and waiting. It smelled the death it had created. The smell fired its rage and fueled its hunger. It craved the feeling of fresh flesh between its yellow teeth. Just above, there was a loud splash. It focused its good eye on the surface of the lake. Its senses began to tingle, tweaked by a new smell—the smell of blood—fresh blood. It swam closer, trailing a few feet behind the new prey. The prey swam slowly, skimming the surface like a fleshy surfboard. The creature closed the gap. It sensed vulnerability. This would be an easy kill.

Minutes passed. The bleeding prey swam. The creature followed. Soon, it would strike and drag its victim down. One powerful jerk and the prey would be torn apart. The creature would attack. The creature would feed.

CHAPTER 34

Nickles was the first to notice. The torso was riding lower in the water, as if something was dragging it down. It would submerge for a few seconds, then pop back into view. He kept one hand on the boat controls and used his other hand to draw the .45.

"Whatsup?" asked Kingfish.

"I think we got a nibble."

Kingfish picked up the shotgun and moved to the stern. "It's testin' us. Gettin' a feel for the bait. Maybe makin' sure it's real."

"That ugly bastard breaks the surface, you open up on it. Don't wait for me."

Kingfish raised the shotgun and took aim. "Way ahead of ya, son."

The first strike shook the boat with a violent, rocking jerk. Nickles bumped the throttle up a notch to offset the drag. "See it?"

"Nope, but that mother must have jaws like a bear trap to hit that hard. It latches on, you hit that throttle wide open so's we can set the hook."

"Got it."

Kingfish watched the tension grow on the cable until it stretched behind the boat like a circus tightrope. It twisted a half turn, then slammed the boat so hard it jerked the hull backwards. "Now," shouted Kingfish.

A three foot wave crested the stern and flooded the deck as Nickles slammed the throttle to full. The turnbuckle twisted, letting out a low, metallic groan as the cable twisted and seized. Something along the hull cracked and the boat lunged forward. The creature's bulbous green and grey head broke the surface. Its undead mouth was clamped around the torso. Strings of rotten meat and bits of cloth dangled from gaps in its razor sharp, yellow teeth.

Kingfish opened up with the shotgun, putting six deer slugs in the monster's mutant face. It tightened its jaws around the torso. Nickles raised the .45 and emptied the magazine. The rounds ricocheted off the yellow teeth. The creature's grip loosened long enough for a hot blast of rancid air to escape from its wet, rubbery lips. A blast from Kingfish's shotgun took off a rotted fin. He reloaded it and tossed it to Nickles. "Try this."

Nickles unleashed a barrage of slugs into the creatures back, tearing out pulpy globs of slimy, green fish flesh. The creature raised up, exposing its entire length. "That damned thing's the size of a mini van."

Kingfish was setting up the Barrett, tossing sandbags around the legs of the bipod to help steady it as he perched it on the deck. He shouted to Nickles over the roar of the engine. "We keep that sucker on the hook long enough, maybe we can blow it apart one piece at a time." He slammed a magazine into the Barrett and cycled the action. "Rock-n-Roll."

Nickles watched Kingfish put five well-placed rounds into the monster's ulcerated flesh. The beast was energized, thrashing to free itself from the hook and cable. Nickles reloaded the shotgun and pumped more slugs into the scaly green flesh above its eyes. The thing kept coming.

"Bullets ain't doin' diddly shit to this thing." Before Kingfish could slam another magazine in the Barrett, the creature veered hard left, the hook twisted deeper into its jaw and the turnbuckle snapped. It was loose. They watched it dive, sending an oily plume of sludge and water high into the air, as monster, hook and cable disappeared below the surface.

"I got a feeling it'll be back," shouted Nickles.

"Yep, it ain't near out of gas just yet."

Nickles eyes landed on the boat's fuel gage. "No, but we are."

"Well, screw that noise." Kingfish abandoned the Barrett and hauled the black case out on the deck. "If I'm goin' down, I'm goin' down swingin' a big stick." He hoisted Ardetta out of the case and grabbed a steel rod.

They waited.

The milky dead eye appeared first, followed by the bullet-riddled head and rotted body. It lurched forward, following the boat.

"Bring it back around," shouted Kingfish. "See if you can get behind it while I draw a bead on it."

Nickles put the boat in a hard turn and circled the creature while Kingfish readied Ardetta. He set the tension, notched up a steel rod and braced himself, locking his legs around the deck rail. Nickles brought the boat around and fell in behind the creature.

"Now goose it and get me in close to that shitbag."

"How close?"

"Right on top of it."

"Are you nuts?"

Kingfish grinned. "It's been said a time or three, yessir."

"Alright, it's your funeral." Nickles punched it. "Hold on to your asshole."

The boat jumped forward, giving Kingfish a clear shot at the thing's mangled body. He took a deep breath, steadied his arms and tightened his fingers on Ardetta's smooth metal trigger. "Say howdy-do to my sweet Ardetta you undead maggot." He squeezed the trigger. The steel rod left Ardetta with a whoosh, knifed into the lake and punched through the monster's rotted ribcage. It disappeared beneath a shower of putrid fish bits and tainted lake water. "Bullseye."

Nickles kept a hand on the throttle while he watched the water thrash and churn. They circled the spot where the thing had gone down. On the third pass the water had calmed, leaving nothing but shredded fish and an oil slick. "You think that undead thing is finally dead?"

"Has to be. Ardetta, she ain't never let me down yet."

Nickles face went ashen as he pointed to an oil slick forming on the water. "Guess there's a first time for everything."

Kingfish turned in time to see the monster's riddled head emerge, then its ravenous mouth broke the surface, gaping and hungry and seeking revenge. "Well kiss my fat, flabby, ass."

CHAPTER 35

Nickles gave the throttle all it had as the most gave chase. "We got about five minutes of fuel left. Any more bright ideas?"

"Just one." Kingfish reached into his lockbox and pulled out a tightly wrapped, green bundle.

"What's that?"

Kingfish carefully unrolled the bundle and lifted out a tightly capped, glass jar. "Just a little somethin' I threw together for emergencies." He sat cross-legged on the deck and placed the jar between his legs. "Just hold the boat steady as you can, this shit ain't all that stable."

"Now you tell me." Nickles tightened his grip on the controls. "Mind if I ask what's in it?"

"Bein's you're a law dog, I don't think you wanna know."

"Yeah, I do."

Kingfish pulled a condom from his pocket, unrolled it and began filling it with the contents from the jar. When he was done he knotted the end. "The exact formula's a little sketchy. It's part hydrogen peroxide, a touch of acetone and a little nitric acid. The technical name for it is Triacetone-Triperoxide. I call my concoction 'jerkwater' and it's as a redhead with a belly full of Jack-n-cola."

"Where the hell do you come up with this stuff?"

"Hey, like I told ya, I ain't just some dumb redneck."

"And you aim to try and blow that thing up with a rubber full of 'jerkwater'?"

Kingfish fiddled with a huge brass knob on the back of Ardetta. "Any luck at all I will. Just gotta lower the tension so's the steel rod goes in and stays put till the jerkwater takes over."

"And if it doesn't?"

"Then we gonna die watchin' one hell-of-a fireworks show."

"How you plan on setting it off?"

Kingfish pointed to the shotgun. "That's where you come in." He turned the brass knob another full turn, then taped the loaded condom on the steel rod with a strip of duct tape. "I aim to put this right in that bastard's rotten hide. Once it sticks to its smelly innards, you pop that rubber with as much double aught buckshot as you can pump in there."

Nickles loaded the shotgun with double aught and racked the action. "You ever done anything like this before?"

"Whatta you think?"

"I think we're fucked."

"Not if me and Ardetta got anything to do with it."

The monster swam closer.

Kingfish took aim. "Ya ready?"

"No."

CHAPTER 36

The creature was disoriented, but intrigued. It was use to being the hunter, not the hunted. Something was fighting back. The challenge of a clever, resistant prey energized the monster. The smell of fear wafted over the lake and permeated its fluttering, undead gills. The scent was tantalizing. It wanted flesh. It wanted death. It wanted revenge.

The holes through its deformed skull and rotting flesh exposed jagged shards of fractured fish bones. There was a heaviness tugging at the thing's jaw. It felt nothing but the maddening urge to kill and feed. The ravenous mouth opened wide. There was a sickening metallic crack as yellow teeth connected with the dangling length of cable and severed it cleanly in two. The pressure on the thing's jaw eased. The grappling hook remained in place, pierced through rubbery lips and decaying jaw muscle. It thrust its mangled body forward, swimming in the direction of the scent.

CHAPTER 37

Nickles kept the boat steady and the throttle wide open. He checked the fuel gage. It was pegging on 'E'. The creature was closing in. Soon it would over-take them. "Whatever we're going to do, we'd best be doing it. We're sucking vapors and that thing's coming like a bat-out-of-hell."

Kingfish double-checked the condom, raised Ardetta and sighted on the monster's head. Nickles shouldered the shotgun, ready to unload on the 'jerkwater' the minute Kingfish delivered the payload. The steel rod left Ardetta with a muffled whoosh, arched over the prop wash and slammed into the creatures head. "Pour it on," Kingfish shouted.

Nickles cut loose. The first two rounds drifted left, missing the 'jerkwater' by less than an inch. He adjusted and fired two more rounds—high and to the right.

"Come on, man, you got this, now take him out."

Nickles racked the action, took a deep cleansing breath and let it out slow. The thing lunged. Nickles fired. The water behind the boat exploded.

Kingfish eased his grip on Ardetta and kissed her sleek metal frame. "Wham, bam, thank ya ma'am!"

Chunks of putrid fish rained down, filling the deck with smelly, undead shrapnel and shattered yellow teeth. The boat rocked violently. Weapons and ammo rolled across the deck and tumbled overboard.

Kingfish spun around in a victory dance, hugging Ardetta to his chest and shouting at the top of his lungs. He teetered on the edge of the bow and jabbed a finger at Nickles. "Ya see? I am and always *will be* the King. You can't lock me up and you can't get rid of me. You need me out on this lake. Admit it, Charlie Nickles, after today, you *want* me out on this lake."

Nickles watched Kingfish's performance with amusement. He beat his chest and leaned out over the water to scoop up rancid hunks of exploded monster and chuck them high into the air. He heaved a glob at Nickles and reached for another fistful. That's when it happened.

It rose from the froth in a smooth, swift arch. Its snapping mouth surrounded Kingfish's torso and clamped down hard. The force cleaved Kingfish in half as Nickles' eyes went wide with terror. He reached for the throttle, but the engine was gone—died of fuel starvation. He backed as far away from the bow as he could get and aimed the shotgun at the biggest snapping turtle he had ever seen. Its shell was fractured, its head rotted and it stared at Nickles with one dead, milky eye and a mouthful of Kingfish.

As it slipped beneath the surface, Nickles pulled the trigger on an empty shotgun. Then, it was gone. Nickles stood among the blobs of zombie fish and rot, remembering what Kingfish had said about the Adena out on the lake. *"Appears as if the clans in these parts were right partial to the fish and the turtle. They were sacred idols used in blood rituals."* Nickles stumbled to where

Ardetta lay on the bloody deck. He picked her up, found one of Kingfish's steel rods, loaded her as he'd seen Kingfish do, and waited.

CHAPTER 38

Charlie Nickles floated adrift on Vivid Valley Lake for six hours, clutching Ardetta tightly and waiting for the mutant turtle to return. It never came, but he knew it was out there, carrying the Adena curse in its blood and a vicious, insatiable hunger under a shell the size of a circus tent.

When the docks at J & K Tours came into view, he propped Ardetta next to the rail and rummaged through Kingfish's gear till he found an oar. It was warped and split, but it would have to do. He thrust it into the water and began to paddle. Two hours later he reached the docks. He was sweaty, exhausted and covered in rotted fish and Kingfish's blood. He climbed the ladder, took three steps and collapsed in a heap.

"Jeez, Mister, you stink somethin' awful."

Nickles struggled to pull his eyes into focus, to see where the voice was coming from and who was speaking. There was a flash of red and the smell of something sweet and syrupy. He rubbed his eyes and looked again. There was a Richmond Roosters ballcap, a catsup stained T-shirt and a freckled face stuffed with cotton candy.

"Well, Mister, was I right? Was it pirates?"

Nickles raised up on an elbow. He narrowed his eyes and stared out over the water to that small, distant, bloody spot where Kingfish had met his fate.

The kid was persistent. He tugged at Nickles' bloody pants leg. "Mister? Hey, Mister? I said, was I right? Was it pirates?"

There was a cold breeze gusting off the lake, blowing in a dense, gray fog. Nickles wiped the sweat from his brow with a shaking, bloody palm. "I wish it were, buddy. I wish it were."

The kid kicked the toe of Nickles' bloody boot with his black high-top sneaker. "You're no fun. Nothin' good ever happens here. Not in Vivid Valley."

CHAPTER 39

Twenty miles east of Grant's Cove, deep in the woods, a rusty Ford pickup pulled to a stop next to a log cabin. A husky figure with a heavy limp stepped onto the porch. His face was shrouded in darkness. He waited for the driver to cut the engine and crawl out of the truck. "Kendall, my main man, anybody see you pull in?"

"Nope."

"And you weren't followed?"

"Nope."

"You right sure of that?"

Kendall rummaged through a cardboard box in the bed of his truck, angry at the rapid-fire questions. "Hell yeah I'm sure Parker. I ain't no damned fool. I've made the run a thousand times or more. I know what's what, and then some."

Parker limped closer, his pock-marked face now visible in the dim light leaking through the single cabin window. "Took ya long enough. Where ya been?"

"Hit a snag."

"Musta' been a damned biggin', ya been gone a couple days."

Kendall took a deep breath and stared out into the dark woods. "Ran afoul of that idiot deputy again."

"Deputy Hogan, Sheriff Pid Riley's trained ape."

"The one and only."

Parker took a hobbled lap around the porch, dragging his bum leg over the splintered boards. "We square with him?"

Kendall drummed his fingers on the edge of the truck bed. "If you call three gallons of moon bein' square."

"Thought the deal was for two."

"Always has been."

Parker gave him the 'what gives' look.

"Seems Hogan's got him a serious case of the goo, said the price for keepin' quiet done went up."

"Gotdanged if every swingin' Sam in this valley ain't got some kinda' racket goin'. It keeps up, Vivid Valley's gonna get a nasty reputation. So, whatudya tell that dipshit deputy?"

Kendall stopped drumming his fingers. "I told him to fuck off. He said he had no problem with that. He said he'd be happy to fuck off over to Riley's office and fill him in on the whole shebang."

"Ya mean 'cept the part about him bein' on the take."

"Exactly."

"Does that leave anything for us?"

"Whatta you think?"

Parker slapped his hands together. "Well, alright, son, let's get to it."

Kendall pulled a gallon jug from the box and stepped up onto the porch. "That bastard Hearld Money pulled the same stunt he tried last time we made the run."

Parker grinned through brown, rotting teeth. "Tried to jack the price on ya, did he?"

Kendall placed the plastic jug on a rickety wooden table. They each assumed their usual positions, flopping down in aluminum lawn chairs and propping their mud-crusted boots on the wobbly porch rail. "He's a sneaky little prick," said Kendall. "I'll give him that much."

Parker nodded, eyeing the jug. "Whadja do?"

"I slapped the cash in his grubby palms and gave him my best take-it-or-leave-it face."

"And?"

Kendall let out a wet snort. "He took it."

They licked their lips, broke out a pair of tin cups and cracked the seal on the jug.

Parker held up a filthy, cautionary hand. "Wait, better let that breathe a minute."

Kendall eyed the empty tin cup anxiously. "Yeah, right." He filled his cup, gripped it with both hands and took in the liquid with one noisy gulp. "Sheeee-it!"

"Smooth?"

Kendall knitted his brows and pulled his lips into a crooked pucker. "We gonna need to have a talk with 'Ol Hearld Money. This here batch of moon is a bit off."

"Whatcha mean?"

"Its kindly got a bitter taste."

Parker filled his cup and took a long blast. "Woah, it does have a wicked bite to it, don't it?"

Kendall cleared his throat and hocked a loogie into the bushes surrounding the cabin. "Smells sour too."

"Whatcha expect? It's sour mash, ain't it?

Kendall emptied his second cupful and refilled it from the plastic jug. "Money usually does a fine job with his double purified bust-head." He took another long sip and stared into the cup. "This here batch? I don't know, it kindly disappoints."

"Relax. You're just pissed 'cause you had to drive over to that rundown old barn and haggle with that drunken fool."

"I 'spose you're right."

"Course I am, now drink up."

"Rumor is, he sinks this stuff in Vivid Valley Lake to cure it and keep it cool. Ya think that's true?"

Parker shrugged. "Beats the hell outta me, but it makes for a good story, don't it?"

"Yeah, it does add to the mystique, huh?" Kendall downed his third cup, refilled it and eased back in his chair. "You know that silly old shit swore he had a Bigfoot stompin' around over there behind his barn."

Parker let out a barking laugh. "Shit, Kendall, if y'all put away as much homemade corn liquor as he has, you'd be seein' every ghoulish monster this here world has ever cooked up."

"I guess, but he's right sure this thing's been runnin' around slaughterin' his chickens, killin' dogs, attackin' critters in the woods, even molestin' his cattle."

Parker sipped at his moonshine. "I got me a bit of a theory 'bout Hearld."

"Whatsat?"

"I reckon there'll come a day, somebody'll find him face down in a pile of manure or floatin' in the shallows over at that damned lake, his belly full of booze and his lungs full of water."

Kendall grunted and scuffed a muddy clod off his boot sole. "Maybe one of them butt-ugly monsters he's always seein' will sneak up on him and gobble his ass up."

"Wouldn't that be a hoot?"

"It would for a fact."

The two men set about drinking in earnest. Soon they were laughing, hooting and trading off-key chorus's of a Hank Williams medley. The corn alcohol began to take hold, setting its hooks in their addled brains and loosening their tongues. The world slowly began to spin.

"Kendall, I believe you was off a note or two on that last verse."

Kendall's muddy boot slipped off the porch rail. "Wasn't neither, I was beltin' out Hank Williams when I was still poopin' yellar."

"More like belchin' it out." Parker began nodding off, his chin bumping his chest. "You's still outta tune though. Ain't no denyin' that. I could tell it, right off."

"Wasn't."

"Was."

The boozey bickering continued. Neither man noticed the tiny hole in the plastic jug—a hole that had let Money's moon seep into Vivid Valley Lake and undead graveyard juice to leach back in. After the fifth cup, Kendall's jaw began to throb. He felt a dull ache building at the back of his mouth. He elbowed Parker. "You awake?"

Parker groaned and lifted his head. His left eye was swollen, coated with a milky, white film. "Don't feel so good."

"Can't hold yer liquor, can ya?" Kendall yawned. His jaw cracked. A jagged, yellow tooth rolled off his tongue and bounced across the porch. "Feels like they's a monster in my mouth fightin' to get out."

"Lightweight." Parker rocked back in his lawn chair and scratched his head, A clump of hair and rotting flesh tore loose from his scalp and stuck to his fingers. He stared at the mess in his hand and laughed. Tell ya what, I'm bone tired. I gotta catch a few Z's."

"Umm Hum."

"I feel like I could sleep the sleep of the dead."

Kendall leaned forward and spat out another jagged yellow tooth. "Good night. Don't let the critters bite."

—END—

About Murphy Edwards

Murphy Edwards is the award winning author of Serious Money, Bumper Music, Heavy Weather, Noodlers, Mister Checkers, Ace of Spades and The Last Days of Maxwell Sweet. His dark and deadly fiction has appeared in Trail of Indiscretion, Hardboiled Magazine, Big Pulp, Criminal Class Review and in the anthologies Dead Bait, Dead Bait II, Dead Bait III, Assassin's Canon, Abaculus II & III, Night Terrors, Unspeakable, Bloody Carnival, Indiana Horror 2011, Indiana Horror 2012, Grave Robbers, Serial Killers Iterum, Hell and Indiana Science Fiction 2012. Edwards is the 2011 recipient of The Midwest Writers Workshop Writers Retreat Fellowship Award for Fiction and is the Co-Editor of Indiana Crime 2012 and Indiana Crime Review 2013. Contrary to popular belief, Edwards does not suffer from ichthyophobia. He currently docks his trawler at:
http://murphyedwards.wordpress.com
www.facebook.com/murphy.edwards.96

Made in the USA
Charleston, SC
16 February 2014